KT-374-129

MY SISTER THE VAMPIRE

VAMPALICIOUS

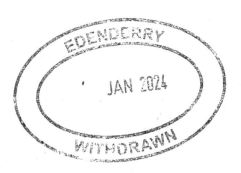
EDENDERRY

JAN 2024

WITHDRAWN

Sink your fangs into these:

Switched

Fangtastic!

Revamped!

Sienna Mercer

MY SISTER THE VAMPIRE

VAMPALICIOUS

EGMONT

With special thanks to Josh Greenhut

For Mercury, who keeps me rising

EGMONT
We bring stories to life

My Sister the Vampire: Vampalicious first published in Great Britain 2009
by Egmont UK Limited
239 Kensington High Street
London W8 6SA

Copyright © Working Partners Ltd 2009
Created by Working Partners Limited, London WC1X 9HH

ISBN 978 1 4052 4372 8

3 5 7 9 10 8 6 4 2

A CIP catalogue record for this title is available from the British Library

Typeset by Avon DataSet Ltd, Bidford on Avon, Warwickshire
Printed and bound in Great Britain by the CPI Group

All rights reserved. No part of this publication may be reproduced,
stored in a retrieval system, or transmitted, in any form or by any means,
electronic, mechanical, photocopying, recording or otherwise, without
the prior permission of the publisher and copyright owner.

Chapter One

Ivy Vega and her best friend, Sophia Hewitt, hustled through the oldest cemetery in Franklin Grove on their way to school on Monday morning. The grassy path, stiff with frost, crunched loudly beneath their heavy boots, and Ivy pushed her hands into the pockets of her full-length, black down jacket to keep them warm.

I'm going to miss this old graveyard when I move to Europe, Ivy thought. Even though it was still a little dark, in the distance she could make out the low silhouette of her boyfriend's family crypt, where she and her friends had spent so much time hanging out. Outside the cemetery gates, the lights of nearby houses twinkled.

'Such a killer party!' Sophia exclaimed, interrupting Ivy's thoughts. It seemed like forever ago, but on Saturday, Ivy's human twin, Olivia, had been initiated into the vampire community, and they'd had a little celebration. 'You must be seriously excited,' Sophia went on, 'that Olivia knowing about vampires isn't a secret any more. It's all over the World Vide Veb.'

Ivy pressed her mouth down into her black knitted scarf and exhaled, warming her neck. *That's not the only thing that isn't a secret any longer*, she thought. 'Sophia,' she said aloud, 'there's something I have to tell you.'

🦇   🦇   🦇

Olivia Abbott was met by a hot blast of indoor air as she opened the huge oak front doors of

Franklin Grove Middle School. Scanning the lobby, she pulled off her hat and swung it around by one of the pink pom poms that hung from its earflaps. She jumped up and down to get the cold out. Olivia had worn her cheerleading uniform for a school spirit assembly, but even with leggings, she felt like a popsicle.

Where are you, Camilla? Olivia thought as she hopped from foot to foot, keeping her eyes peeled for her friend. *I have huge news!*

The door to the outside swung open, and Olivia looked over eagerly. Unfortunately, it was just Charlotte Brown, Olivia's snotty cheerleading captain. She was wearing fluffy white ear-muffs.

'Hi, Charlotte,' Olivia said, unable to keep the disappointment out of her voice. Charlotte let the door swing shut behind her, but her cheerleading cronies, Katie and Alison, hurried in on her heels. They were wearing ear-muffs too.

'Oh, Olivia, I'm so totally cold!' Charlotte whined.

'We're cold too!' said Katie and Alison, who had a talent for always thinking the same thing as Charlotte.

'Then you'd all better get inside right away and warm up!' Olivia said, switching on her smile. They skipped past without another word.

One person trickled into school after another, and every time the door to the outside opened, Olivia's heart leapt. Finally, she caught sight of Camilla's bouncy blonde curls.

'Camilla!' Olivia called.

'Hey,' Camilla said, her face breaking into an easy smile when she saw Olivia. 'Sorry I'm a little late. You sounded so excited on the phone last night. What's up?'

Olivia grinned. 'Only the biggest news of my entire life!'

Camilla looked at her sceptically. 'Bigger than finding out you have a long-lost twin sister?'

Olivia wrinkled her nose; Camilla had a point. Olivia and Ivy hadn't even known they each had a twin until Olivia's first day of school in Franklin Grove a few months ago. Come to think of it, the whole 'my-sister-is-a-vampire' thing was big news too, but of course Camilla didn't know anything about that. Olivia was one of the only humans in the world who did.

'Just as big,' Olivia decided, pulling Camilla behind the enormous potted ferns in the corner of the lobby.

Olivia took a deep breath. 'You can't tell anyone,' she said. 'Promise?'

'Promise,' Camilla said solemnly. 'Just tell me already!'

🦇　　　🦇　　　🦇

'I *am* telling you,' Ivy protested.

'No,' Sophia said, 'what you're doing is *trying* to tell me. So far you're just sighing a lot.'

Ivy sighed again, sending a tiny cloud into the cold air. 'I still can't believe it,' Ivy murmured by way of explanation.

'Ivy,' Sophia said sternly, 'I'm freezing my fangs off here.'

'You don't have fangs,' replied Ivy, peering around the cemetery to make sure no one else was lurking nearby. 'You file them like the rest of us.'

'It's an expression,' Sophia said, her voice rising with frustration. 'Now tell me your big revelation!'

'I found . . .' Ivy gulped. 'Olivia and I found out . . .'

Sophia stared at her impatiently.

'Who my real father is,' Ivy blurted at last.

'Really?' Camilla cried, her eyes widening. Olivia nodded, biting her lip to contain her smile. 'I'm so happy for you!' Camilla threw her arms around Olivia, accidentally knocking one of the ferns. Olivia giggled.

'I knew you and Ivy would find some answers if you kept looking,' Camilla said proudly.

Olivia had to admit that their perseverance had paid off. She and her sister had been trying to solve the mystery of who their parents were since they'd first realised they were twins.

'Thanks, Camilla,' Olivia said, hugging her again. 'I wanted to tell you in person.'

'So who is he? Who's your dad?' Camilla asked, her voice bursting with curiosity.

Olivia pursed her lips, savouring the moment.

Camilla read her face. 'I knew it!' she squealed. 'It's a celebrity! I always thought you two had George Clooney's lips!'

'Nope,' Olivia shook her head coyly. 'Even better.'

'Antonio Banderas?' Camilla whispered in awe.

'Well, then, who?' Sophia said excitedly, wrapping her arm around Ivy's as they made their way out of the cemetery.

Ivy's long dark hair fell in front of her face. 'He's, uh, his name is . . . Karl Lazar,' she sputtered. *Why am I having so much trouble telling my oldest friend the whole story?* Ivy wondered. Somehow, this was just too unbelievable to blurt out.

'Lazar?' Sophia repeated. 'You mean that Transylvanian vamp aristocrat who fell for a human?'

Ivy nodded dumbly.

'That's amazing! Do you know if he's still alive?' Sophia asked.

'Oh, he's alive,' Ivy said.

'How do you know?' Sophia pressed.

'He's been in hiding for the last thirteen years,' Ivy answered.

As Franklin Grove Middle came into view in the distance, Sophia's steps slowed. 'Ivy, why do I think there's something you're not telling me?'

Ivy smiled shyly, relieved that her friend knew her so well. 'Because there's something I'm not telling you?' she replied.

As Sophia searched her face, Ivy took one last deep breath. She pushed her hair out of her eyes. 'My dad is my dad,' she announced, the words rising into the air like smoke.

Sophia looked at her blankly.

'My dad is my *real* dad,' Ivy clarified.

Sophia did a double-take. 'You mean your father, Charles Vega, who you've known for your entire life . . .'

'. . . is Karl Lazar,' Ivy finished.

Sophia peered at her in disbelief. 'You're biting my neck, right?'

Ivy grinned. 'No fangs, remember?'

🦇   🦇   🦇

'But why would Mr Vega pretend to be Ivy's adopted dad when he's actually her real father?' Camilla asked.

'We don't know,' Olivia frowned. 'Maybe because he didn't want Ivy to know she had a twin.'

'But why not?' Camilla pursued.

All Olivia could do was shrug. She wanted to tell her friend everything she and Ivy had learned: about how their father was a vampire while their mother was a human, and that he'd separated the twins after their mother had died. But she'd taken a Blood Oath never to violate the First Law of the Night, which meant she must never reveal the existence of vampires to a non-vampire. It was a bummer, because Camilla was supersmart, and Olivia thought maybe she'd have some ideas about why Mr Vega had done what he had.

🦇   🦇   🦇

Ivy and Sophia climbed the school steps. 'Does your dad know you know?' Sophia asked.

Ivy shook her head. 'Olivia and I talked about it and agreed that we're not telling our parents yet. Olivia's mom, Audrey, is going to flap like a bat when she finds out the truth. And my dad's already utterly uncomfortable around Olivia.'

They went inside and were walking across the lobby when Ivy heard someone call her name in a stage whisper. She looked around, but none of the students milling around the lobby was looking her way.

'Ivy! Sophia!' the voice came again.

'I think that fern is calling us,' Sophia

murmured, pointing to the corner. The two of them walked over. Suddenly, a pink-nailed hand reached out and pulled Ivy behind the greenery.

Olivia was huddled back there with Camilla.

'Did you tell her?' Ivy and Olivia asked each other at the same time. They nodded to each other and then had a big group hug.

'Congratulations on finding your father,' Camilla grinned at Ivy.

'Can you believe that, this whole time, their real dad's been right in front of them?' Sophia said excitedly to Camilla, who shook her head in disbelief.

'You guys can't tell anyone,' Olivia said seriously.

'Not even Brendan?' asked Sophia.

'Except Brendan,' Ivy replied. She was planning on telling her boyfriend after first period. She wanted to tell him in the science hallway, where he'd first asked her out. She'd made him a card, thanking him for all his support during her search for the truth.

'Must be a big secret,' smirked Sophia. 'After all, we're hiding behind a fern!'

For once, Olivia didn't smile. 'Ivy and I are declaring a state of emergency; she and her dad are supposed to be moving to Europe.'

'He's your dad, too,' Ivy reminded her gently.

Olivia nodded. 'Right,' she agreed, thinking that that was going to take some getting used to. 'And we've got less than ten days to convince him not to move.'

'We're not going to let ourselves get split up again,' Ivy declared bravely.

'And I'm *not* losing my biological father now that I know who he is,' Olivia added.

Camilla and Sophia had both snapped to attention. 'How can we help?' Camilla asked.

13

'Do you really think your dad might change his mind?' Sophia wondered, scratching her head through her winter hat.

'He has to,' Ivy answered.

'We're going to come up with something that will make it impossible for him to leave,' said Olivia.

'Something so killer,' Ivy put in, 'that he'll be dying to stay.'

'Like what?' asked Sophia.

Ivy and Olivia looked at each other doubtfully. 'That's what we're hoping you'll help us figure out,' Ivy smiled weakly.

The four girls stared at each other. They were still standing there, deep in thought, when the bell for first period rang.

'Huddle,' Olivia called, and the four of them gathered close. 'We'll meet at lunch to come up with a plan,' she said.

Everyone nodded. Then Olivia prompted everyone to put a hand in the middle. 'Franklin Grove or Bust,' she said.

'Franklin Grove or Bust!' Ivy and her friends repeated in unison, their hands pumping and then rising into the air like a starburst.

Chapter Two

After third period, Olivia was redoing her Natural Sky eye shadow in her locker mirror when she spotted Sophia hurrying down the hall out of the corner of her eye.

'Codeword,' Sophia said meaningfully, her chunky digital camera swinging around her neck.

'You mean Code Black?' Olivia asked, referring to Sophia and Ivy's secret lingo for an emergency meeting in the science hall bathroom.

'No,' Sophia shook her head. 'Code*word*.'

Olivia tucked her eye shadow back into her

purse. 'But I don't know the codeword,' she said quizzically.

'Not codeword,' Sophia said, rolling her black-lined eyes. 'Code *Word*. Code *Word*.'

Olivia stared at her. 'You Goths can be really cryptic sometimes, you know that?'

'Code Word,' replied Sophia, lowering her voice to a whisper, 'means we're meeting in the library.'

'I thought we were meeting in the cafeteria,' Olivia said, slamming her locker shut.

'We were,' Sophia said as Olivia followed her down the hall. 'But Ivy changed the plan.'

'Does Camilla know?'

'Ivy's bringing her,' Sophia explained. 'They just had gym together.'

'But why? What's Ivy up to?' Olivia wondered.

'Beats me,' said Sophia. 'I'm just the messenger bat.'

The entrance to the library was at the end of a wide hallway near the principal's office, and Ivy and Camilla were waiting by the door. Ivy stepped forward and handed Olivia a carrot. With the other hand, she gave Sophia a piece of beef jerky that was as red as licorice.

'What's this?' Olivia asked.

'Lunch,' said Ivy matter-of-factly.

'We have work to do,' Camilla declared.

Olivia looked at the carrot and took a begrudging bite. *Just because vampires call humans 'bunnies', that doesn't mean we live on carrots*, she thought.

As Olivia and Sophia snacked, Ivy explained her plan. 'There's nothing my father likes more than a well-researched report. He's always giving these killer presentations to his clients about what he wants to design for them. So I thought, why not prepare our own report to convince him not to move?'

'What would it be about?' Olivia asked with her mouth full.

'How much better Franklin Grove is than Europe,' Ivy answered.

Sophia swallowed her last bite of beef jerky and shook her head. 'You think Franklin Grove is better than Europe?' she queried incredulously. 'Europe has the Eiffel Tower.'

'Which people can fall off of,' Ivy countered.

'It has the fashion shows in Milan,' pointed out Olivia.

'Which create an unhealthy self-image for girls everywhere,' argued Ivy. Camilla nodded vigorously.

Sophia clearly wasn't convinced. 'So what, exactly, does Franklin Grove have that Europe doesn't?'

'That's easy,' Ivy said, her dark eyes sparkling.

'*Us.*' With that, she spun on her boot heels and pulled open the library doors.

Olivia couldn't help smiling. *Well*, she thought, charging into the library after her sister, *it's worth a shot.*

🦇   🦇   🦇

Ivy marched up to the librarian's desk and found a woman wearing dark lipstick and stylishly chunky black and green glasses, hunched over an enormous book about the Middle Ages.

'Is Mr Collins here?' Ivy asked.

The woman looked up from her book. 'Mr Collins moved to Nashville to play country music. I'm Miss Everling, the new librarian.' She stood, held out her hand and pumped Ivy's enthusiastically. Everyone introduced themselves. 'Killer sweater,' the librarian said to Sophia, whose top was embroidered with the branches of a bare, crow-filled tree.

You're the new librarian? Ivy thought, impressed.

'Hopefully you can help us, Mrs Everling,' said Olivia.

The librarian put her hands on her hips. 'It's Miss. Anyway, shoot.'

'We're doing a presentation on Europe,' Camilla piped up.

'Europe, huh?' Miss Everling said, grabbing a pencil off her desk like it was a sword. 'Follow me.'

As she walked, Ivy noted Miss Everling's striped black-and-white leggings and her grey corduroy skirt. *I wonder if she's a vamp*, she thought.

'Welcome to Europe!' announced Miss Everling, arriving at an aisle near the back of the library. She ran a wine-red fingernail along the spines of some glossy paperbacks. 'Want to dance the night away in Barcelona? Ski the Alps? Drop

21

out of school and live large for twenty-five dollars a night?'

The girls all stared at her.

'Jok-ing,' Miss Everling sang. 'I'm a *school librarian*, remember? But we do have a very impressive selection of travel guides,' she concluded.

'Do you have any books on what's bad about Europe?' Sophia asked.

Miss Everling stared at her. 'Nothing's bad about Europe. I travelled there for a whole year after college.' Her eyes rolled toward the ceiling, and she sighed dreamily. 'So much culture and history—'

'History?' Ivy interrupted with a meaningful glance at her friends.

Olivia followed her train of thought exactly. 'Yeah, didn't Europe have the Black Plague?'

'And both those world wars,' Camilla

pointed out with a grimace.

Miss Everling frowned. 'Time out,' she said, peering at the girls over her lenses. 'What's this project about again?'

Ivy fiddled with one of the books on the shelves. 'We're trying to convince our . . . friend . . . not to move to Europe,' she said carefully.

Olivia nodded enthusiastically. 'We have to make this person see that Franklin Grove is totally better.'

'Oh, now I understand,' Miss Everling said softly. 'My best friend moved to California when I was thirteen. It's so hard saying goodbye.'

Seriously, thought Ivy sadly.

Miss Everling tapped her pencil against her dark lips thoughtfully. She gestured to the camera hanging around Sophia's neck. 'Do you have pictures of your friends on that thing?'

'Of course,' Sophia replied.

Miss Everling adjusted her glasses. 'Don't worry, ladies,' she said. 'I'm going to help you make a pitch your friend won't be able to resist. Something exciting. Something emotional. Something that truly sucks!' She winced at her impulsive use of vampire slang. 'I mean, something really great.'

Miss Everling is the deadliest librarian ever, Ivy thought, exchanging excited looks with her friends.

'So,' Miss Everling said, 'when is this important project due, so to speak?'

'Today,' Ivy replied.

Miss Everling started to protest, but Sophia said, 'Our friend's supposed to move in ten days.'

'We don't have any time to lose!' Olivia pleaded.

'OK, OK,' Miss Everling said. 'Then we'll need to split up. Who wants to research Franklin Grove?'

'I'll do it,' Olivia volunteered. 'I just moved here a few months ago, so I could stand to learn a thing or two.'

'Good,' said Miss Everling. 'The local history section is by the copying machine in the corner. Camilla, how would you like to do Europe?'

'Roger, Queen Informasys!' Camilla said, saluting. Ivy had no idea what that meant – Camilla was always making obscure references to sci-fi books she was obsessed with.

'A Coal Knightley fan, huh?' Miss Everling grinned. 'Isn't he the greatest? Anyway, Captain Omega, your mission is to find unappealing pictures of Europe. It won't be easy. Start with these travel guides, and then check out the European history section, just like you and Ivy were thinking.'

'You two –' Miss Everling pointed her pencil at Ivy and Sophia – 'follow me to the computers.

I'm going to show you how to make a digital slideshow that's guaranteed to make your friend laugh and cry. But, more than anything, it's going to make her *stay*!'

At 4:30 that afternoon, Olivia stood behind her sister on the front porch of Ivy's enormous house atop Undertaker Hill. They'd stayed after school with Camilla and Sophia, rushing to finish their presentation, and it looked totally awesome. But as Ivy reached for the doorknob, Olivia was suddenly filled with dread. 'Wait,' she blurted.

Ivy stopped. Olivia turned and looked down on Franklin Grove; amid the fog and the bare December trees, she could just make out the roof of the school in the distance.

'Do you really think this could work?' she wondered nervously.

'Why? Don't you think the presentation's killer?' Ivy asked quickly.

'I do. I really do,' admitted Olivia. 'But when my own dad decided to come to Franklin Grove for a new job, I begged him not to move. There was nothing that would change his mind.'

'Except my dad loves Franklin Grove,' Ivy said. 'He always has. And while Europe's a killer continent, I don't want to spend the rest of eternity in some boarding school in Luxembourg.'

'OK, but that doesn't mean he loves . . .' Olivia's voice trailed off before she said the word 'me'. She'd barely seen Mr Vega since finding out he was her father. The initiation with the Vampire Round Table meant that she'd been officially accepted into the vampire community, but even afterwards he'd remained completely awkward around her. *He doesn't even like being near me,* she thought.

'Maybe you should do the presentation without me,' Olivia said aloud.

'You have to come,' Ivy said. 'You're the best public speaker.'

'I know, but he's never really seemed to . . . *like* me very much.' Olivia bit her lip doubtfully. 'If I'm his daughter,' she said, her eyes starting to mist over, 'then why doesn't he love me? Is it because I'm human?'

Ivy's eyes softened and she shook her head. 'Our mom was a human like you,' she said gently. 'She was the love of his life.'

'So what happened?'

'I don't know, Olivia,' Ivy admitted. 'Something that made him a separationist, more wary of mixing with humans. He changed. But that means he can change again.'

Olivia sighed deeply. 'It's just . . . I'd give anything to know what it's like to have him as a member of my family, you know?'

'You will,' Ivy assured her. 'But first we have to convince him not to move away.'

Olivia nodded and took a deep breath, determined not to let her sister down. 'You're totally right,' she said.

Ivy grinned encouragingly, gave Olivia a quick hug, and opened the door.

They found Mr Vega hunched over his desk in his study. Ivy crept in while Olivia stayed back near the doorway. Even from across the room, she could see that he was sketching something with a piece of charcoal.

'Hey, Dad,' Ivy announced.

'Oh, hello, Ivy,' Mr Vega said, bolting to his feet. 'I didn't hear you come in.' He shuffled his drawing under some other sketches.

'Hi . . .' Olivia said, momentarily unsure how to address the man before her, '. . . Mr Vega.'

'Hello, Olivia,' Mr Vega responded stiffly, not having noticed her standing in the door until that moment. He quickly averted his eyes, and Olivia's heart sank.

'What are you working on?' Ivy said.

'Nothing,' he said. 'Just some design ideas.'

'My dad designed this whole house himself,' Ivy told Olivia proudly.

Olivia already knew, but she guessed Ivy was just trying to remind her dad of that fact. She tried to say something enthusiastic, but she was tongue-tied. 'Cool,' she croaked at last.

'Each wall, each floorboard, each light switch, each shelf,' Mr Vega said nostalgically. 'I am going to –' He stopped himself abruptly.

'Miss being here?' Ivy finished his sentence,

her dark lips curling into a grin.

'Yes,' Mr Vega said. 'Yes, of course. But a house is not a good enough reason to stay,' he added quickly.

'There are lots of other reasons,' Ivy said. 'Right, Olivia?'

Olivia felt the familiar sensation of stepping in front of a crowd. She was still wearing her cheerleading outfit, after all. Her nervousness magically dissolved and she felt her voice bubble into her throat. 'That's right, Ivy!' she agreed. She reached into her backpack, pulled out the CD with their presentation on it, and held it out with a stellar smile. *Time to cheer our hearts out!* she thought.

🦇   🦇   🦇

'Please, Ivy,' her father pleaded as Ivy shooed him from his chair and slid the CD into his computer. 'I am really very busy.'

'Too busy for the most important presentation of your entire life?' Ivy retorted. Her fingers were shaking as she grabbed the mouse, but she was determined not to let either her dad or her sister know how nervous she was. 'You can go sit over there.'

'This won't take long, Mr Vega,' chirped Olivia. 'You won't regret it. Promise!'

No matter what, Ivy thought gratefully, *Olivia always rises to the occasion.*

Defeated, Ivy's father collapsed into the reading chair across from the desk. Once she had the presentation cued up, Ivy spun the blank screen all the way around so her father could see, and then she and Olivia went around to the front of the desk and arranged themselves on either side of the screen.

'Ready?' Ivy whispered.

'Ready,' Olivia smiled, squeezing her hand.

Ivy reached behind them and clicked the mouse to begin, and the first plaintive guitar notes of *Paint It, Black* by the Rolling Stones sounded from the computer's speakers. Between Ivy and Olivia, a tiny speck appeared in the middle of the blank screen.

'I love this song,' Mr Vega remarked approvingly.

Ivy couldn't help rolling her eyes. 'I know,' she said out of the corner of her mouth as the white speck grew larger and larger, like a meteor approaching from outer space.

'Shhh!' scolded Olivia as the title slammed to the front of the screen, accompanied by a sudden barrage of drums.

'THE MOST IMPORTANT PRESEN-TATION OF YOUR ENTIRE LIFE,' Olivia and Ivy read in unison.

Ivy's dad let out a small laugh. 'I thought you were only saying that,' he said.

Olivia stepped forward professionally. As Mick Jagger sang 'I see a red door and I want to paint it black', the screen dissolved into an old black-and-white etching of some modest huts that Olivia had found in a library book. 'The year is 1666,' she began. 'A small band of Transylvanian exiles settle on a very special piece of land. They decide to name it Franklin Grove.'

Ivy was seriously impressed that her sister had memorised her lines. Ivy had tried, but she'd ended up having to write notes on her palm. 'That same year,' Ivy said, glancing down at her hand, 'across the ocean . . .'

The screen transitioned to a similar woodcut, but this one was of a much bigger city, all its buildings covered with inky flames that licked the air. '. . . the Great Fire of London wipes out the homes of 70,000 innocent people!'

On the soundtrack, there were shouts and

screams. Ivy noticed her father wincing, which she took as an encouraging sign.

'And that,' said Olivia, in an uncharacteristically low voice, 'is merely where the differences begin.'

'Here's what happens at the highest point in Europe,' said Ivy, as the screen showed an avalanche threatening to consume a group of downhill skiers.

'Here's what happens at the highest point in Franklin Grove,' said Olivia, as the screen displayed a stunning picture Sophia had taken of the Vega house at dusk, the wide, crimson sky behind it.

'Here's what happens when people cheer in Franklin Grove,' Ivy went on. The screen changed to a picture of Olivia standing atop a pyramid of Franklin Grove Devils cheerleaders, her fist held triumphantly over her head. Ivy could swear she could see a glimmer of pride in her father's eyes. *It's working!* she thought hopefully.

'And here's what happens when people cheer in Europe,' said Olivia. On screen, a crowd at a soccer match had descended into a chaotic riot.

Now came Ivy's favourite part of the whole presentation. 'Here are the sorts of things that happen if we stay in Franklin Grove,' she declared. The screen started moving from image to image, without any accompaniment other than the rocking chords of the Rolling Stones: Ivy in her wine-colored strapless ballgown, standing with her tuxedoed father's arms around her before the All Hallows' Ball; the black-and-white *Vamp!* magazine picture of Ivy and Olivia, shorn of make-up, looking at each other in the guest bathroom mirror; her father, clapping for Olivia after she passed the Three Trials and was initiated by the Vampire Round Table; Ivy, Sophia, Olivia and Brendan with their arms around each other at Brendan's family crypt; Ivy's father, thoughtful in a chair in the corner of the living room while Ivy and Olivia chatted excitedly before him. The pictures went on and on.

Ivy watched her father's face. She could tell he was moved, his eyes flickering as he leaned forward intently in his chair.

At last, Olivia stepped forwards once again. 'And here, Mr Vega,' she said, 'are the sorts of things that might happen if you go to Europe.'

Suddenly, the soundtrack sped up crazily and its volume rose until it was an unrecognisable, screeching mess. A quick succession of images flashed on the screen: a mustachioed man running from a charging bull, two dinky European cars crashing into each other, a World War Two plane dropping bombs, a wrecked apartment building in France, a soccer player with an agonised look of defeat on his face, a painting of Mount Vesuvius erupting.

The rush of images ended abruptly, along with the unbearable noise. The simple, lone guitar melody from the beginning of the song rang out plaintively, and a single phrase appeared on the black screen: 'Franklin Grove or Europe?'

Ivy and Olivia triumphantly read the final screen that came next: 'FRANKLIN GROVE!'

Ivy's father clapped enthusiastically. His face was flushed, and he had a smile that Ivy realised she hadn't seen in weeks. 'Terrific job,' he said. 'What a wonderful presentation! You should share it with the Franklin Grove Chamber of Commerce.'

I knew he'd like it, Ivy thought. *I knew it would work!* 'So we're not moving?' she blurted.

Her father's smile abruptly fell from his face, like a dark cloud suddenly drifting across a full moon. He dropped back into his chair and studied his hands. Olivia looked at Ivy anxiously.

'Can't you see how much we have here, Dad?' Ivy pleaded.

'Don't go,' Olivia said in a small voice.

'I have to,' Mr Vega whispered. He raised his eyes to them sadly. 'We have to go, Ivy. I know it's difficult for you to accept . . . but you must try.'

Ivy looked at him in disbelief. *Why are you being so stubborn?* she thought. She tried to think of something she could say, anything that might get through to him and make him realise they couldn't go to Europe.

Her father forced his mouth into a strained smile that seemed utterly fake compared to the one from a few moments ago. 'You should try to think of all the good things about Europe,' he said hopefully.

Ivy shook her head. She turned to Olivia. 'I

thought he'd listen to reason. Or emotion. Or *us*,' she said softly. 'But I guess I was wrong.'

Without another word, Ivy led her sister out of the study. She knew Olivia was struggling not to burst into tears, too.

Chapter Three

The next day at lunch with Olivia, Sophia, Camilla and Brendan, Ivy was still in a pitch-black mood.

'My father is being impossible,' she fumed. 'He's determined to move. I'm not sure there's anything I can do that will change his mind.'

'Have you tried biting him on the leg?' said Brendan. 'My little sister Bethany did that once to my dad, and it really got his attention. I mean, he almost had to go to the hospital.'

Ivy couldn't even smile. 'My father doesn't like hospitals,' she said glumly.

Across from her, Olivia moved a piece of limp broccoli around her plate with her fork. 'Do you think he wants to go to Europe to get away from me?' she said quietly to her plate.

Ivy's heart cracked open like a coffin. Sometimes, she forgot that this was just as hard for Olivia as it was for her – maybe harder. 'He wouldn't do that, Olivia,' she said as reassuringly as she could. 'It's the job. It's a really killer opportunity.'

'Didn't he say that they made him an offer he couldn't refuse?' asked Sophia. Ivy nodded.

'But we don't even know why he separated me and you in the first place,' Olivia said, unconvinced. 'Maybe when I was a baby, I bit him in the leg.'

Ivy smiled. 'I don't think he would insist on moving away just because of you, Olivia. He was talking about this job before you even came to Franklin Grove.'

Olivia looked at her gratefully. 'You're right,' she said. 'Sorry, I'm just being completely neurotic.'

'What we need to do is come up with something even a great job can't compete with,' Camilla said.

Brendan nodded, his dark curls flopping in front of his eyes. He was so drop-dead handsome. 'With the right reason, your father will decide to stay,' he agreed.

At that moment, Ivy couldn't imagine being apart from Brendan. She felt herself filling with determination again. 'Then we'll just have to come up with the right reason.'

'Hey, Vega!' a voice called.

Ivy spun around and saw Garrick Stephens and two of his greaseball goons, Dylan Soyle and Kyle Glass, winding their way towards the table. Instinctively, she rolled her eyes. The Beasts were

43

the lamest vampires in the whole school.

'Word in the dirt is that you're skipping town!' Garrick said happily.

'What's it to you?' Ivy said coolly.

'Nothing,' Garrick said, but then he turned and grinned at his friends. 'Nothing at all,' he repeated, wheeling back to face her, 'except that with you gone the three of us are going to rule the school!'

Kyle and Dylan laughed idiotically and waited for Garrick to give them high-fives.

'*As if*,' said Sophia under her breath. 'You tombstones couldn't rule an empty cemetery plot.'

Garrick pretended not to hear. 'So, uh, before you go, why don't you do an article on us for the *Scribe*?'

Ivy stared at him, but he just kept leering at her. 'You're not serious,' she said at last.

Garrick sighed. 'Oh, come on,' he whined.

'Once our new band gets famous, you can say that you knew me when . . .'

Rather than answering, Ivy fixed Garrick with her worst death squint. She imagined she was burning a black hole through the centre of his forehead.

'Fine, but don't think we're going to send any VIP tickets your way,' he grumbled finally, and lumbered off with the other Beasts in tow.

'Gross,' giggled Camilla.

'I can't believe they've started a band!' grinned Olivia.

Sophia tapped the table with a spoon as if it were a gavel. 'I hereby call our second emergency meeting to order!' she announced.

'Second?' said Brendan. 'When was the first?'

I was worried you'd ask that, Ivy thought. 'Yesterday,' she said. 'But it was girls only. Now we're co-ed.'

'Good,' Brendan said. 'Because I don't want to miss a moment with you over the next week.'

Ivy's heart ached, and she took Brendan's cool hand in her own. 'You were studying for your social studies midterm exam,' she tried to explain.

'Social studies!' exclaimed Sophia suddenly. 'That's how we'll keep Mr Vega in Franklin Grove!'

'Homework and pop quizzes wouldn't tempt me to stay,' Camilla said.

Sophia rolled her eyes. 'I mean what we're *learning* in social studies. We just did a whole unit on the Civil Rights Movement, and we had to watch part of that movie *Gandhi*. There's only one way to successfully fight the blatant injustice of racism, British colonial rule, or being forced to move to Europe!'

'And that would be . . .?' Brendan said cluelessly.

'Passive resistance!' blurted Sophia. She looked around excitedly.

'I should've known that!' Brendan slapped his head with his palm. 'I am seriously going to fail this midterm.'

'You mean like a sit-in?' Camilla asked.

Sophia nodded. 'We'll chain ourselves to Mr Vega's car and refuse to move until he changes his mind.'

'That would certainly be dramatic,' remarked Olivia.

'I bet we'd get in the local paper,' Camilla shrugged.

Between her recent interview with Serena Star on national TV and all the newspaper and magazine articles about Ivy and Olivia being long-lost twins, Ivy had had enough media attention to last eternity. 'I don't know,' she said tentatively. 'We'd miss all our exams.'

'We can do it after midterms,' Sophia suggested. 'As long as we start before the actual day of the move, it'll still work.'

'What would we eat?' Brendan wondered.

'We'll bring food,' Sophia countered.

'But what if we run out of food?' Olivia asked.

'Then we'll be on a hunger strike,' Sophia replied matter-of-factly, stabbing the air with a fork. 'That's what Gandhi did.'

'It's pretty cold out lately,' Olivia said, scrunching up her nose.

Sophia seemed to sense the tide turning against her. 'This can work, you guys!' She waved her fork around. 'History is on our side!'

Ivy knew how Sophia could be when she got attached to an idea. She'd cling to it like a bat on its perch – nothing would bring her back down to earth. 'How about this?' Ivy said. 'Passive resistance can be our last resort. If in a week's time we still haven't been able to convince my dad, we'll start the revolution. Agreed?'

'Agreed,' everyone said, Sophia loudest of all.

'I have an idea,' Camilla piped up. 'Have any of you ever seen that old movie about the identical twins who switch places?'

Olivia shook her head. 'Ivy and I don't have to see that movie!'

'It's our life,' Ivy agreed with a grin. The sisters had switched places a few times since they'd met. Sophia even had photos of Ivy in Olivia's outfit at a cheerleading practice, which made Ivy want to be buried alive.

'Yeah, but there's this one part I keep thinking about,' Camilla went on. 'In order not to get separated again, these sisters have to get their parents back together. They have to make them fall in love again.'

Olivia's face brightened, but Ivy frowned. 'That won't work,' she said. 'Our mother's not around any more.'

'Wait a second,' Olivia interrupted. 'Maybe Camilla's on to something. We might not have our mom, but there are tons of eligible women in Franklin Grove we could set your dad up with.'

Sophia shut one eye and pursed her lips. Then she opened her eye and shook her head. 'Nope, I can't see it,' she said. 'I've known Mr Vega for my whole life, and I've never seen him go on a single date.'

'He's shy!' Ivy said, surprised by her own defensiveness. 'He could have a girlfriend if he wanted to.'

'What about Georgia Huntingdon?' Olivia suggested. 'That lady from . . . that magazine.' Ivy could tell her sister was being discreet for Camilla's benefit – Georgia was the flamboyant editor of *Vamp!*

'I don't think that would work,' Brendan said sceptically.

Ivy nodded. Every vamp in America knew Georgia Huntingdon had a very on-again/off-again relationship with a TV soap star.

'We need someone *perfect*,' Ivy said. 'He's our dad, after all.' In fact, Ivy had always thought that the right woman might help her dad relax a little bit.

'So, are we agreed,' said Sophia, 'that the only thing that might be more killer than a killer job is a killer romance?'

'Agreed,' everyone chimed, and Brendan started playing footsies with Ivy under the table. If she was a bunny, she would have blushed.

Instead, the bell rang for the end of lunch.

'The second emergency meeting is now adjourned,' Sophia declared as everyone gathered up their trays. 'Let's go find Mr Vega his Miss Right!'

For the rest of the day, Ivy tried to think of

women who might be a good match for her dad. She kept a running list on the back page of her notebook, where she usually wrote ideas for the school paper.

Valencia De Borg from the Vampire Round Table? Too cold.

The lady at the adoption agency? Too loud.

Marie the florist who specialised in dead flowers? Too *weird*.

The list went on and on, but Ivy couldn't come up with anyone she thought her father would be interested in.

After school, Olivia had to meet with her algebra study group to prepare for midterms. Ivy went over to Brendan's. The door swung open the moment she touched the doorbell.

'Don't let him see you!' Brendan's little sister Bethany whispered in a panic and pulled her inside. For some strange reason, Bethany was wearing enormous aviator sunglasses. She ran to the window, pulled aside the curtain, and peeked out at the street.

'Who?' said Ivy.

'The vampire hunter!' Bethany replied.

Ivy took off her jacket and hung it by the door. 'Seriously?' Ivy asked.

'FREEZE, VAMPIRE SCUM!' a voice commanded. Ivy's stomach lurched, and she turned to look. Standing in the door that led to the kitchen was Brendan, wearing a long trench coat and a yellow hardhat. In his hand, he held an egg beater. He laughed maniacally.

'EEEEEEEEEEKKKKKK!' shrieked Bethany and starting running in circles around the living room. Brendan took straight-legged zombie steps into the room.

From the kitchen, Mrs Daniels called, 'Please use your inside screaming voice, Bethany,' but it didn't seem to have any effect.

Ivy couldn't help smiling as Brendan clomped right up to her.

'Aren't you afraid of the vampire hunter?' he asked with bulging eyes.

Ivy shook her head. 'Nope,' she said.

'Why not?' the vampire hunter demanded.

"Cause I think he likes me,' Ivy replied coyly. *I am going to miss you so much*, she thought. Brendan touched her arm tenderly.

'You get away from Ivy!' screamed Bethany. She charged and kicked Brendan hard in the leg.

'Ouch!' Brendan cried.

Bethany leapt on his back. 'You big mean vampire hunter uglyman!' she shouted.

Brendan winked at Ivy and gave a monstrous roar. He and his sister collapsed on the living-room floor in a wrestling heap. Bethany was jumping up and down on his back, alternately giggling and shrieking, as he grunted and tried to claw at Ivy's foot. Ivy kicked his hand away playfully.

'You show him, Bethany!' she called.

Suddenly, Mr Daniels burst through the front door. 'Eureka!' he cried, his Einstein-like mane of grey hair pointing in all directions. 'Let's celebrate! I've had a major breakthrough!'

Brendan and Bethany both sat up.

Mrs Daniels came rushing in from the kitchen in an apron. 'Marc! Please calm down,' she admonished. 'We have a guest.' She cast a meaningful glance towards Ivy, who was standing by the couch.

Mr Daniels focused his eyes on Ivy. 'Ivy! It's Ivy!' He bounded over and hugged her enthusiastically.

'Um, hi, Mr Daniels,' Ivy said awkwardly, her arms pinned to her sides. 'How are you?'

'How are *you* is the question!' he said, releasing

her. 'How are you a vampire,' he elaborated, waving his hands excitedly in the air, 'while your twin sister is a human?' He puffed up his chest. 'Well, today, Ivy, I found the answer!'

🦇　　　🦇　　　🦇

Olivia made her way through the Meat and Greet Diner. She could see her sister already seated at their usual booth in the corner. Ivy had called her on her cell phone in the middle of study group and said she had to see her right away. She wouldn't take no for an answer.

When Olivia reached the table, her sister leapt up and hugged her quickly. 'My dad's going to be here to pick me up in, like, fifteen minutes,' said Ivy, 'so we don't have much time.'

They slid into the booth opposite each other. 'Let me guess,' Olivia said. 'You found the perfect Mrs Vega?'

'Better,' said Ivy. 'I found the perfect

explanation for *us* – or, rather, Mr Daniels did. He figured out how it's possible for you to be a human and me to be a you-know-what.'

Olivia's heart leapt up into her throat. 'Really?' she squealed. 'What'd he say?'

'Ever since we went to the V-Gen lab,' Ivy explained, 'Mr Daniels has been running all these tests on the samples he took from us.'

'The strands of our hair and stuff?' Olivia asked, remembering all the weird machines to which she'd been strapped.

'Exactly,' confirmed Ivy. 'Anyway, remember how he said they wouldn't have any results for months?'

Olivia nodded.

'Well, he had a huge breakthrough much sooner than he expected!'

'Which is?' Olivia cried.

'Not very easy to explain,' Ivy admitted with a

grimace. 'You know how Brendan's dad talks.'

'Ivy!' Olivia pleaded.

'OK,' Ivy said. 'I'll do my best.' She scanned the table and grabbed the salt and pepper shakers from next to the napkin dispenser. 'Pretend this salt is your DNA,' she said, shaking some on to the table. Then she made a little mound of pepper adjacent to the mound of salt. 'And this is mine.'

'Oh, my goodness!' came a bubbly voice. 'I know you! You're the twins!'

Olivia looked up to see a pale waitress in a butcher's apron smiling down on them. She was tall and thin, with her long black hair pulled back in a ponytail.

Ivy was looking embarrassed, so Olivia smiled and said, 'Nice to meet you –' she glanced at the waitress' nametag – 'Alice.'

'Oh, I don't want to bother you,' Alice blurted.

'I just came to see if you wanted to order anything.' She smiled hopefully down at Olivia.

'Oh, yes, please,' Olivia replied. 'How about a Strawberry Smoothie?'

'And I'll have a Bloody Raspberry Shake,' Ivy put in.

'Be back in a flap,' Alice winked.

Ivy leaned towards Olivia. 'I think she's new,' she whispered. 'Anyway,' she picked up where she'd left off, 'salt and pepper can't mix.'

'You've clearly never made soup,' said Olivia.

Ivy rolled her eyes. 'It's a *metaphor*, Olivia. Human and vamp DNA are incompatible. That's why the two species can't usually breed.'

'Right,' Olivia said sheepishly.

'Mr Daniels said that, in V-Gen's tests, I didn't show any traces of human DNA, and you didn't show any traces of vamp DNA. He couldn't understand how that could be possible, until he remembered what makes us so special.'

'Our incredible coolness?' Olivia joked.

Ivy smiled and shook her head. 'The fact that we're *identical twins*,' she said. 'Which means we both started in the same embryo.'

Olivia shrugged. 'So?'

'So Mr Daniels thinks that somehow the cells in the embryo became polarised. All of the vamp cells went to one end,' Ivy said, using the blunt edge of her knife to push the salt away from the pepper, 'and all of the human cells went to the other.'

Suddenly, Olivia got it. 'And then the embryo split into two babies!' she gasped.

'One vamp and one human,' Ivy pronounced triumphantly. 'Mr Daniels said the odds are like a billion to one!'

Olivia's heart did a triple handspring. *We're not a mistake*, she thought. 'We're a miracle!'

Just then, Alice returned with their drinks. Olivia and Ivy waited until she was gone before clinking glasses. 'To us!' they toasted.

'You should have seen Mr Daniels,' Ivy went on as Olivia slurped her smoothie. 'He was so excited. When I thanked him for figuring all this out, he said *he* was the one who should be grateful. He wants to write his next book about us!'

'First Serena Star, then the Franklin Grove papers and *Vamp!* magazine, and now a book,' marvelled Olivia. 'We should get an agent!'

'As if,' Ivy smiled and rolled her eyes. Olivia knew Ivy had always hated the spotlight, but, no matter what her sister said, Olivia suspected that she was starting to enjoy the attention just a little bit.

Suddenly, Ivy's face tightened. 'There's my dad,' she said. She hunched over and sucked up the rest of her Bloody Shake in one gulp. Olivia stared into the pink froth of her smoothie.

'Hello,' Mr Vega announced.

'Hi,' Olivia and Ivy said together.

'Are you ready to go, Ivy?' Mr Vega asked.

All at once, the joyous rush Olivia had felt at Ivy's news melted away. She felt like she'd been doing a magnificent aerial cheerleading move, only to discover at the last moment that there was no one there to catch her. What did it matter how she came to be in this world if her own father wouldn't acknowledge her?

She wanted to ask her father why he didn't seem to care about her, but the diner wasn't the right place for that. Instead, she just raised her hand in the air and waved limply to Alice. 'May we please have the check?'

Olivia, Ivy and Mr Vega said nothing as they waited for the bill.

After a minute, Alice brought it over and

slapped it on the table. 'Here you go!' she said. 'Thanks so much. Really, you girls were a pleasure to serve. You have an energy, you know?'

Alice turned to trot away, but Mr Vega cleared his throat. 'Pardon me,' he called.

Alice spun around. 'Yeah?'

'Do I know you?' he said. 'I feel certain that I have seen you before.'

Olivia couldn't believe her ears. *That almost sounds like a pick-up line!* she thought.

Alice screwed up her lips and rolled her eyes around, like she was trying to see the inside of her head. 'Nope,' she said after a second, 'I don't think – WAIT A MINUTE! Have you been to any parties at the art museum?'

Mr Vega's face bloomed into a smile – a real one, not one of those close-lipped pretend smiles Olivia was used to. 'Of course. We met at the last exhibition opening,' he said. 'You're the artist who does those sculptures.'

'I am indeed!' said Alice. Out of the corner of her mouth, to the girls, she added, 'I've never been recognised before.'

Olivia and Ivy just stared at Alice and their father, totally speechless.

'I've always had a passion for our little museum,' he said. 'I remember one of your pieces well. The eight-legged clown.'

'It was a mime, actually,' Alice corrected with a smile.

Olivia kicked Ivy under the table. *She's the one!*

'Olivia and I have to go to the bathroom,' Ivy blurted.

Olivia hurriedly reached into her bag and found a five dollar bill. 'Thank you so much, Alice,' she said, slapping the bill on the table. 'Keep the change.'

'Thanks,' said Alice.

'Dad, I'll see you in the car,' Ivy called over her shoulder as she and Olivia rushed to the ladies room.

The moment they were inside, Olivia peered under the stalls. They were empty. 'Do you think she's, you know,' Olivia said, 'one of you?'

'This is one of our establishments, and she's wearing black nail polish,' Ivy replied. 'So, yes!'

'It's perfect,' declared Olivia. 'She's an artist . . .'

'. . . and he's artsy,' finished Ivy, sounding awed.

'I know!' squealed Olivia. 'And it sounds like he even *likes* her art!'

'Let's invite her over for dinner,' Ivy said quickly.

'Can we do that?' Olivia asked, but her sister was already out of the door. They crept along the bathroom hallway and peeked around the corner to see if Mr Vega was still in the restaurant.

'He's gone,' Ivy whispered, and together they made a beeline to where Alice was standing by the cash register.

'Hi, Alice,' they both said.

'Hi, again,' said Alice.

'I'm Ivy, and this is Olivia,' Ivy said. 'That guy you were talking to – he's my father.'

'Really?' Alice said with a glimmer in her eye. 'He looks so young!'

'He's a widower,' Olivia noted.

'Want to come over to our house tomorrow night?' Ivy offered. 'You could . . . talk about . . .'

'Art?' Olivia suggested.

'Are you girls tugging my wings?' Alice said with a worried look as she twirled her dark ponytail.

Uh-oh, thought Olivia. *We're coming on too strong.*

Alice's mouth burst into a smile. 'Because I'd *love* to!'

Chapter Four

At lunch the next day, Olivia scanned the cafeteria for her friends. She spotted Camilla and Sophia at a table by the windows, hunched over in intense conversation. *Looks like they're still conspiring!* Olivia thought, grateful that her friends were continuing to take Ivy's move so seriously.

'I think,' Camilla said loudly to Sophia as Olivia trotted up, 'that the *Scribe* should run more editorials.'

'I disagree,' Sophia replied. 'I think two is enough. Why – hello, Olivia.'

'Hey,' said Olivia, setting down her tray. *I guess they don't have to conspire* all *the time*, she thought to herself.

Camilla looked at her watch. 'Gotta go!' she said. 'I have a study session for English.'

'Me too!' said Sophia. 'I, uh . . . I have to go work on a piece for my art exam.'

'Really?' said Olivia, trying not to sound disappointed that she was being left alone only a few seconds after she'd sat down. 'What are you doing?'

'What?' said Sophia.

'What's the piece you're working on for your art exam?' Olivia explained.

'It's a painting . . . I mean, a photograph. It's a painting of a photograph?' Sophia said, like she wasn't sure.

'Still trying to figure it out, huh?' said Olivia. 'I know the feeling.'

'Exactly!' said Sophia, lifting her tray. 'See you later, Olivia.'

Olivia started eating her strawberry yogurt. She had just pulled out her algebra book and was trying to get some studying done when Charlotte Brown came up with Katie and Allison.

'You're all alone,' Charlotte moaned, her lower lip pushed out in an exaggerated pout.

'That's so sad!' said Katie and Allison.

Olivia marvelled at how well the two of them could speak in unison.

'You know you can always sit with us, Olivia,' Charlotte said. 'Us cheerleaders have to stick together, right?'

'Totally,' said Katie.

'For sure,' said Allison.

'I guess so,' Olivia said after a moment.

'Awesome!' squealed Charlotte. 'So you'll sign our petition?' Katie slapped a piece of paper filled with signatures next to Olivia's tray. Allison carefully placed a pink pen on top of it.

'Petition for what?' Olivia asked.

'We want to outlaw wearing black to school during the month of December,' Charlotte explained.

'Excuse me?' said Olivia, raising her eyebrows.

'Black is so anti-holiday spirit,' said Katie seriously.

'Plus it depresses everyone during exams!' chimed Allison.

Olivia peered over the edge of the table. 'What about your shoes?' She asked, pointing to Charlotte's heeled black loafers.

Katie and Allison gasped dramatically.

'Shoes don't count,' Charlotte blurted.

'Really?' Olivia eyed the piece of paper beside her tray. 'Does this petition say that? Because my favourite winter boots are black.'

Katie and Allison stared at their captain like they were waiting for her to call a cheer. Charlotte was struggling to come up with an explanation when Ivy and Brendan appeared with their trays and sat down.

'What's that?' Brendan asked, indicating the piece of paper.

'It's a petition banning shoes during December,' Olivia answered matter-of-factly.

'It is not!' cried Charlotte, stamping her foot.

'Who would sign that?' Ivy wondered.

Charlotte turned bright red. 'NORMAL PEOPLE!' she shouted.

Everyone at the surrounding tables turned to look.

'*Relax*, Charlotte,' whispered Katie, totally embarrassed.

Charlotte sneered at Ivy. 'I'll be so happy when you move,' she seethed, 'and I get a regular next-door neighbour instead of a drab bag like you.'

'Drab bag,' Ivy said, savouring the words. 'I sort of like that.'

At which point Charlotte *hmmphed*, snatched her petition off the table and stormed off with her friends.

'You know what they say,' Olivia said, bursting out laughing. 'If you can't join 'em . . .'

'Beat 'em!' grinned Ivy. She and Olivia bumped elbows.

'You twins are dangerous,' marvelled Brendan.

'Olivia,' said Ivy, 'I was just telling Bren about how the next phase of our plan is a go.'

'You mean Operation FANGED?' said Olivia. Her sister blinked cluelessly. 'Friends Against Needlessly Going to Europe in December!' she clarified.

Ivy laughed.

'I actually think the acronym for what you just

said is FANGTEID,' Brendan said sceptically, pronouncing it 'fang-tide'. Olivia threw a napkin at his head, but he easily batted it away.

'So you asked if it was OK to have Alice over for dinner?' Olivia asked Ivy.

'Not exactly,' Ivy answered. She let her hair fall in front of her face, which Olivia knew meant she was trying to hide. 'I told Dad that someone's coming over as part of a final art project that you and I are working on.'

'What kind of art requires a waitress from the Meat and Greet?' asked Brendan dubiously.

'Performance art?' Ivy tried.

'The art of romance,' Olivia corrected, batting her eyelashes.

'Brendan,' said Ivy, pushing her hair out of her face. 'Do you want to be the waiter? You could wear the tux you wore to the All Hallows' Ball. You looked drop dead in it.'

Brendan frowned. 'I can't,' he said apologetically. 'I promised Bethany I'd take her to see the HB.'

'What's the HB?' asked Olivia.

Ivy glanced over her shoulder to make sure no one could overhear. 'The Holiday Bat,' she whispered.

Olivia looked at her sister blankly.

'You know how human kids think Santa Claus magically comes down the chimney on Christmas Eve and leaves presents for them?' Ivy asked.

Olivia nodded.

'Well, we don't have Santa. We have the HB.'

'One winter, a bat flew out of my parent's chimney,' Olivia remembered. 'My dad chased it out of the door with a tennis racquet.'

'Hmm,' said Brendan, 'I bet he got lousy Christmas presents that year.'

'Actually, I gave him a really nice tie,' Olivia protested.

'Does he ever wear it?' Brendan asked, raising his thick eyebrows meaningfully.

Come to think of it, thought Olivia, *no, he doesn't.*

'Oh, stop it,' Ivy interrupted. 'The HB is a myth.'

'Try telling Bethany that,' said Brendan. 'She's been begging me for weeks to take her to the mall so she can sit on the HB's back and tell it what she wants for Christmas.'

'That is so cute!' cried Olivia. 'I want to see the HB. It'll be my first vampire Christmas.'

Ivy shushed her. 'Can you lower your voice, or do you want us all to get staked?' she hissed. 'And we're not going to the HB,' she added. 'We're too old.'

Olivia started to protest, but Ivy said, 'Olivia, we have much more important things to focus on right now. Like going to my house after school to prepare the romantic meal that's going to save my life!'

'Don't you worry about tonight,' Olivia said confidently. 'Alice is so totally perfect. It'll be love at first bite.'

Brendan chuckled, but Ivy still looked sceptical.

'I got the two of you together, didn't I?' Olivia pointed out.

Brendan and Ivy looked at each other. 'The bunny has a point,' he said.

🦇   🦇   🦇

Ivy stood at the kitchen counter, frantically flipping through her father's *Taste of the Night* cookbook as Olivia peered over her shoulder. They only had a few hours before Alice arrived.

'How about "Tortellini with Red Sauce",' Olivia suggested. 'That sounds good.'

Ivy scanned the recipe and shook her head. 'We don't have goose's blood.'

'Gross,' said Olivia under her breath.

Ivy spotted a recipe for rare beef lasagna and asked Olivia to look in the pantry for lasagna noodles.

'Ew!' Olivia cried after a moment. 'There's a box of powdered blood jell-o in here!'

'That's my dad's favourite,' Ivy said. She spun around to look at her sister. 'Do you think it's fancy enough for dessert?'

'I know how to make a sweet cream topping from scratch,' Olivia offered. She came over and plopped a box of lasagna noodles on the counter.

'Perfect,' said Ivy. 'Now, all we need is an appetiser.'

'How about a soup?'

As Ivy flipped back to the front of the cookbook, she remembered their conversation at the Meat and Greet the previous day. 'Killer idea,' she grinned. 'After all, we already have salt and pepper.'

An hour later, Ivy had just put the lasagna in the oven when she heard the front door open.

'Ivy,' her father called, 'I'm home!'

'In the kitchen!' Ivy called back.

When he saw them, his father dropped his briefcase with a thud. *I can't believe he's still so shocked by the sight of Olivia*, thought Ivy.

'What have you girls done to my kitchen?' he gasped.

'Hi, Mr Vega,' Olivia said, awkwardly wiping her hands on her apron, leaving bright red stains.

Ivy surveyed the situation. The counter was covered in blood paste and flour, and there were dirty bowls and spoons and pans on every available surface. As if on cue, the pot of water on the stove boiled over with a hissing burst of steam.

Ivy gulped. 'Olivia and I are working on our art project,' she said.

'*This* is your art project?' her dad demanded.

Ivy nodded. 'We have to make something for someone else, so we're making dinner.'

'Well, then, I'd better leave you two artists to your work,' her father said tentatively, slowly turning on his heels to leave the kitchen.

Olivia cleared her throat. 'Mr Vega? It's sort of supposed to be a special occasion, so you might want to dress up a little bit.'

'What kind of special –'

'See you in an hour!' Ivy interrupted, and before her dad could say anything else, she waved him out of the door with the backs of her hands like she was shooing a bat.

Ivy and Olivia were lighting the candles in the middle of the dining-room table when the pipe-organ doorbell rang.

'Girls!' Mr Vega's voice called faintly from upstairs. 'The door!'

Ivy was about to go and answer it, but Olivia grabbed her arm. 'Lesson of Love Number One: interaction is the key to attraction,' Olivia whispered.

'What does that mean?' Ivy asked.

The doorbell rang again. '*He* should get it,' Olivia said.

Good idea, thought Ivy. 'DAD! CAN YOU GET THE DOOR, PLEASE?' she yelled. She snatched a black lacquer plate off the table. 'WE HAVE OUR HANDS FULL OF PLATES DOWN HERE!'

A moment later, Ivy could hear the faint patter of her father descending the grand staircase.

Ivy and Olivia peeked around the corner into the foyer just as their father reached the bottom of the steps. His hair was slicked back, and he was wearing pin-striped black pants and a tailored white shirt under a grey blazer. *Perfect!* Ivy thought.

'Any woman would totally fall for him,' Olivia whispered.

'Sorry to keep you waiting,' Ivy's father apologised as he opened the door. 'Alice!' he exclaimed.

'It's Charles, right?' Ivy heard. 'Like the prince?'

Ivy's father stood there, speechless.

Invite her in, Ivy pleaded silently.

'Please, come in,' her father said.

'Thanks!' Alice said and charged into the foyer. She was wearing an enormous crocheted sweater dress, with black leggings and silver legwarmers. On her head was a black faux-fur trapper hat. *She looks like a dancer in a Russian music video*, Ivy thought.

'Creative outfit,' Olivia whispered hopefully.

Ivy's father snapped his head in their direction like he'd heard. He locked Ivy in his gaze, and his eyes widened.

We're staked! Ivy thought.

Rather than ducking out of sight, though, Olivia pushed past Ivy and marched into the foyer. 'Hi, Alice!' she smiled. Ivy nervously hurried after her. 'Thanks so much for helping out with our art project!'

Alice screwed up her lips. 'I thought I was here for dinner.'

'You are,' Olivia said. 'We had to create something special for someone else, so we're making dinner for you and Mr Vega!'

'That's art?' Alice looked confused.

'That was my question exactly,' Ivy's father said stiffly.

'I usually work in papier-mâché,' Alice admitted.

'It's *performance art*,' said Ivy, pulling out the only explanation she had.

Alice's eyes lit up. 'Oh! I love performance art! Don't you, Charlie?'

Charlie? thought Ivy. *No one calls my dad Charlie.*

'I once painted my whole body white,' continued Alice, 'curled up in a ball, and hung myself from the ceiling for a piece. I called it "The Phases of My Moon".'

Ivy's father smiled uncomfortably.

As she and Olivia led the way to the dining room, Ivy heard Alice say, 'Wow, Charlie, your house is so enormous and ultra-conservative modern. You should really consider metallics!'

Good sign, Ivy thought. *She's interested in interior design.*

Olivia and Ivy pulled out the two chairs opposite each other at the oak dining-room table, which was strewn with dead rose petals

atop the black silk tablecloth.

'There are only two places,' their father said, clearly surprised. 'Won't you girls be joining us?'

'We can't,' Ivy said firmly.

'It would totally defeat the purpose,' added Olivia. 'You know, of our art.'

Ivy was grateful when Alice brushed past her dad and took a seat. 'Did you girls fold these napkins to look like bats?' she asked. 'The Japanese say that origami is the purest art form.'

'Yes,' Ivy's father admitted, taking a seat at last, 'that is a lovely touch.'

'Make yourselves comfortable,' said Olivia.

'And we'll be back in a moment with your first course,' added Ivy.

As her sister ladled soup into black lacquer bowls, Ivy peeked into the dining room. Her father and Alice were chatting amicably. Alice was leaning forward, her chin resting in her hands, her eyes gazing up at Ivy's father.

It's working! Ivy thought.

🦇　　　　🦇　　　　🦇

Everything's going perfectly! thought Olivia. Through the crack in the dining-room door, she could see the candlelight flickering warmly on Alice and Mr Vega's pale faces. Both of them were wolfing down their cream of plasma soup. As she ate, Alice talked about waitressing at the Meat and Greet – the enormous walk-in freezer ('Like a cave!'), how hard it was to find comfortable shoes ('If people like us can live forever, why do we still have back pain?'), how tips were divided ('Evenly'). Mr Vega smiled and nodded attentively.

'Anyway,' said Alice, 'I think Ivy and Olivia are absolutely, 100 per cent right on. Serving food is an art!' Mr Vega continued to nod silently.

He didn't say anything as Alice finished the last roll.

Uh-oh, Olivia thought. *Silence*. She turned and bumped right into her sister, who'd been peering over her shoulder the whole time.

'How come no one's talking?' Ivy whispered.

'Lesson of Love Number Two,' Olivia replied softly, 'never let an awkward moment linger.' She rushed to the counter, grabbed the bottle of sparkling white blood cells that was chilling there, and slipped into the dining room.

'So,' she said as she topped up the wine glasses, 'you're both actively involved with the Franklin Grove Art Museum. I've never been.'

'You've never been?' Mr Vega and Alice both repeated incredulously.

'Olivia, you must go,' Mr Vega said. 'It is an excellent museum, one of the best in this part of the country.'

'When Charlie's right, he's right,' Alice said, raising her glass in the air before taking a gulp.

'Really?' said Olivia. 'What's your favourite piece of art there, Mr Vega?'

Her father's eyes shifted as if he was imagining that the piece of art was right there in the room with them. 'There is a piece of sculpture on the first floor that takes my breath away,' he said.

'Which one?' asked Alice.

'It is a late work by Carlos Van Thacter, a Transylvanian artist,' Mr Vega replied. 'An enormous black granite spike rises from the floor, as if from the centre of the earth. And then it bends, gracefully, almost like a blade of grass. For me, it illustrates the struggle between the natural and the unnatural.'

'You mean that big black thing by the elevators?' Alice said. 'I've always found that cold and boring.'

'Cold and boring?' Mr Vega repeated. 'Well, it might not be one of those cartoon collages on the second floor that everybody –'

'My friend, Marie, made those,' Alice interrupted.

Olivia slipped back into the kitchen.

'Why are they fighting?' Ivy demanded.

'They're not fighting,' Olivia said, though she wasn't sure. 'They're having an intellectual debate.'

'Well, you have to stop them!'

'What do you want me to do?' Olivia asked.

'Clear their plates and change the subject,' Ivy commanded and pushed her sister back through the swinging door. Olivia almost stumbled right into the back of her father's chair.

'May I take that?' she panted, gesturing to Mr Vega's bowl. 'So, Alice,' she said, searching her mind for a harmless subject for conversation, 'how long have you lived in Franklin Grove?'

'Three and a half years,' said Alice. 'I used to live in Paris. I just love Europe!'

Olivia couldn't help wincing. A pan clattered in the kitchen.

'It's nothing!' called Ivy.

'Oh?' said Mr Vega to Alice, clearly interested in hearing more.

The two of them spent the entire main course talking about Europe, pausing only to rave about Ivy's lasagna. In the kitchen, Olivia whipped heavy cream with sugar and vanilla in a huge ceramic bowl. 'It's fine, it's fine, it's fine, it's fine, it's fine,' she chanted to herself as she whipped.

'Will you please stop saying that?' Ivy said in a deflated voice.

'It's true,' Olivia answered. She was determined to remain optimistic.

'If the whole purpose of tonight was to

convince our father *not* to move to Europe,' Ivy said, 'how is them talking the whole time about Europe fine?'

'Because it shows just how much they have in common,' said Olivia. *If they like each other*, she thought, *he'll stay. He has to!*

After she cleared their main-course plates, Olivia prepared to bring out dessert. 'Lesson of Love Number Three,' she announced, 'set the mood.' She turned down the lights in the dining room and put some harp music on the stereo. Then she carried out a big bowl of grapes, plus the two dishes of blood jell-o, topped with her special whipped cream.

'Dessert is served,' she said smoothly, placing the dishes carefully on the table.

'You girls have really outdone yourselves,' Mr Vega said, seeming genuinely impressed. He took a bite, and his eyes lit up. 'This topping,' he said.

'It's cream, with sugar and vanilla, right?'

'Made it myself,' Olivia answered proudly.

Mr Vega looked at the dessert longingly. 'I once knew someone who would have loved a sweet topping like this. I haven't had anything like it in years.' He fixed Olivia with a pained smile. 'Thank you.'

'Enjoy your desserts,' Olivia whispered. She knew, somehow, that he had been talking about her mother.

She took a deep breath as she re-entered the kitchen.

'How's it going?' Ivy asked.

'They're totally falling for each other,' Olivia said, trying to convince herself. 'There's no way he's going to want to move now.'

Suddenly, a huge crash sounded from the dining room. Olivia and Ivy looked at each other and rushed through the door.

Mr Vega was standing behind Alice, his arms wrapped around her in a bear hug. Alice's eyes looked like they were about to pop out of her head.

Is this some strange vampire hugging ritual? Olivia wondered.

Mr Vega squeezed, and Alice emitted a sickly sound that culminated in a *pop*. A small purple orb the size of a marble sailed out of Alice's mouth and splatted on the wall behind Olivia's head.

Alice breathed deeply. 'If I were human, you would have just saved my life!' she said, turning and throwing her arms around Mr Vega's neck.

He looked at Ivy and Olivia over her shoulder. 'Alice choked on a grape.'

'Are you OK?' gasped Olivia.

'We never should have served grapes,' Ivy blurted.

'No, no,' Alice said. She shifted Mr Vega

around awkwardly, her arms still around his neck. Now *she* was facing them over *his* shoulder. 'I'm not upset,' she smiled beatifically. 'This man is my hero!'

Olivia exchanged open-mouthed looks with her sister. *We did it!*

A half-hour later, she and Ivy were peeking around the corner of the foyer, spying on Alice and Mr Vega again.

'Thank you, Charlie,' Alice cooed. 'I had such a terrific time. You have very strong arms, you know.'

'It was certainly an eventful evening,' Mr Vega answered.

'Maybe some time we can go to the museum together and I can teach you a thing or two about art,' Alice suggested.

Mr Vega gave one of his close-lipped smiles. Alice came right up close to him.

Kiss her! Olivia wanted to yell. *Kiss her!*

Instead Mr Vega said, 'Bye now,' and gently pushed Alice out the door. Beside Olivia, Ivy slumped to the floor in defeat.

Mr Vega turned towards where they were hiding. 'You can come out now, girls,' he called.

Uh-oh, thought Olivia. She recognised the tone of his voice: it was the one used by parents everywhere to indicate when you're in big trouble.

'Thanks for participating in our art project, Mr Vega,' Olivia said hopefully as she and Ivy came out into the open.

He walked towards them. 'If this were an art project,' he said, 'you two would get an A. Tonight was creative, unexpected and memorable. And really, Ivy, the lasagna was superb.'

'Thanks, Dad,' Ivy said.

'But as a date,' he sighed, 'I would have to give

it an F. Even without the Heimlich Manoeuvre.'
He looked at them sternly. 'This wasn't an art
project, was it?'

Olivia and Ivy both shook their heads.

'Alice is a lovely person and a talented
artist, but I am perfectly capable of choosing
my own dates. In any case, there's no point
in my starting a relationship when we're about
to move.'

'But that's exactly why we –' Ivy began to say,
but Olivia stopped her with a look.

It's no use, Olivia thought sadly.

'Olivia, I'll drive you home now,' Mr Vega said.
The conversation was over.

During the car ride, Olivia sat staring straight
ahead, thinking about how miserably her plan
had failed. Next to her, she could hear Mr Vega
occasionally sighing as the streetlights illuminated
his pale face.

This sucks, she thought, and she didn't mean it in the good way vampires did.

Chapter Five

The next day at lunch, Olivia slapped her tray down and slumped into a chair.

Brendan eyed her suspiciously. 'Wait a minute,' he said, looking from her to Ivy. 'Did you two switch again?'

'No, Brendan,' Ivy rolled her eyes.

'He's right.' Sophia studied Olivia's face. 'The real Olivia would never sulk like this.'

Ivy blinked with frustration. 'That is the real Olivia!' She waved her black-nailed hands in front of Sophia's face. 'And I'm the real Ivy!'

'Likely story,' said Brendan, unconvinced.

'Will you please tell them, Olivia?' Ivy begged.

Something surged through Olivia's chest, like a crowd doing the wave. 'AREN'T I ALLOWED TO HAVE A BAD DAY?' she shouted.

Everybody stared at her, speechless.

'Sorry,' Olivia said softly, wrinkling her nose. 'Ivy probably already told you that last night was a total failure.'

'It's OK,' Sophia said gently. 'There's always chaining ourselves to Ivy's mailbox.'

'It was a good plan,' Olivia said stubbornly. 'Even if Alice wasn't the right girl, there must be someone in Franklin Grove our father could fall in love with!' She angrily broke a celery stick in half, and Brendan flinched. 'We could try speed dating. We could hold a singles party. You people have online dating services, don't you? There has to be something we can do!'

'Olivia,' Ivy said, reaching across and touching

her hand gently. 'It's a dead end. Even if we had a vamp goddess, we don't have enough time to make a romance work. Besides, Dad would see it coming from a mile away.'

Olivia nodded grudgingly. She knew her sister was right.

Brendan tapped the table with his fork. 'As the only male member of Operation FANGED,' he said, 'I hereby pronounce Plan B . . .'

'Dead,' they all said together.

'Time to come up with Plan C,' Ivy said hopefully.

Aren't I usually the optimistic one? Olivia thought. 'While we're coming up with plans,' she said, her throat suddenly dry, 'can we come up with one to get me out of tonight?'

'Why? What's happening tonight?' Ivy enquired.

'My mom got me a surprise,' Olivia winced.

Suddenly, she realised that she had the worst headache ever. 'She sprang it on me this morning. We have two tickets to see a show tonight.'

Ivy looked confused. 'I thought you love the theatre.'

'I do,' said Olivia. 'Just not shows with flying monkeys in them.' Saying the words 'flying monkeys' sent a horrible chill down her spine.

'Flying monkeys?' Ivy turned to Sophia and Brendan, but they both shrugged. 'Olivia,' she said finally, 'did you take Bethany's VitaVamp again?'

Olivia shook her head and a heavy sigh racked her body. 'I'm seeing *Wicked: The Musical.*'

'Isn't that like *The Wizard of Oz*?' asked Brendan.

'Yes, but from the witch's point of view,' Sophia told him. 'How deadly is that? That show sold out ages ago!'

'I'd *kill* to see *Wicked*,' moaned Ivy.

'Well I'd kill *not* to,' said Olivia weakly. 'I saw *The Wizard of Oz* once, when I was eight years old, and I've had nightmares ever since.'

'What kind of nightmares?' asked Sophia.

'That witch,' croaked Olivia, 'and her monkeys.'

'You mean the winged things dressed as bellhops?' Brendan quipped.

Ivy hit him in the arm, as if to say, *This is serious.* 'So if it gives you nightmares, why are you going, Olivia?' she asked.

'Because my mom's convinced it will help me,' Olivia explained. 'She blames herself for letting me watch the movie when I was little. She thinks that because this show's all about the nice side of the witch, it will end my suffering, or whatever.'

'Your mom is taking you to see a musical as *therapy*?' Brendan laughed.

'It's not funny!' Olivia snapped. 'Once I

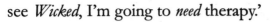

see *Wicked*, I'm going to *need* therapy.'

'Come on, Olivia,' said Sophia. 'You're not going to –'

'I'll FREAK!' Olivia cried hysterically. She pressed her sweaty palms into the table. 'That witch and her monkeys,' she said again in hushed terror.

'Can't you talk to your mom?' asked Ivy.

Olivia closed her eyes. Her headache was getting worse by the millisecond. 'That's the worst part. She's all pleased with herself for finally finding a way to help me "heal the wounds of my childhood". It would break her heart if I didn't go.' She opened her eyes, and her head throbbed. 'Can someone help me?' she squeaked.

Ivy's lips curled into a smile. 'I can.'

Olivia's vision cleared slightly. 'How?'

'We'll switch!' Ivy announced.

All at once, Olivia's headache lifted.

'You can be me at my house, packing boxes for the move,' Ivy explained, 'and I'll be you and go see *Wicked*.'

'You would do that?' Olivia gasped.

'Yes,' Ivy said, sighing as if a great burden had been placed upon her, 'I would be willing to see a sold-out musical I've always wanted to see if it would help my beloved twin sister avoid emotional distress.'

Brendan and Sophia groaned.

'Having an identical twin rocks!' Olivia exclaimed. Suddenly she realised she was thirsty and starving. She chugged the glass of water on her tray and popped the celery she was holding in her mouth.

'No kidding,' Sophia teased. 'Too bad you can't hire your switching services out to those of us who are less fortunate.'

'That would be a killer job,' Ivy admitted.

Killer job. The words stuck in Olivia's head. Suddenly, a light bulb went on. 'That's it!' She swallowed her celery. 'That's Plan C! That's what will convince your dad to stay in Franklin Grove!'

'A twin he could switch with?' guessed Brendan.

'No,' Olivia said. 'A job even better than the one he's leaving for.'

Ivy's eyes widened. 'You are a genius,' she cried.

'Yeah, but I try not to brag,' giggled Olivia.

Ivy was already on her feet, stacking her plates on her tray and gathering her books. Olivia and their friends rushed to do the same.

At that moment, Camilla appeared with her lunch in a brown paper bag. 'You're not all leaving, are you?' she asked.

'Yeah,' said Ivy, 'but so are you, Camilla.' She spun Camilla around and pointed her towards the doorway.

'But where are we going?' Camilla said.

'To look for a job!' replied Olivia, taking her friend's arm.

They walked into the library two minutes later. 'Well, if it isn't the Anti-European Bloc,' said Miss Everling, coming out from behind her desk. 'Did your friend decide to stay in Franklin Grove?'

'Not yet,' replied Ivy.

'Aw.' Miss Everling kicked the ground with one of her tight leather knee-length boots. 'I was sure that presentation would work.'

'We still haven't given up, though,' Sophia added resolutely.

'That's the spirit,' Miss Everling said. 'How can I help?'

'Do you have the local want ads?' asked Brendan.

'We've got all the county and state papers,'

Miss Everling smiled. 'To the periodicals!' she commanded.

A minute later, Miss Everling had left the four of them gathered around the latest edition of the Franklin Grove *Gazette* splayed open on a table. Camilla was bent over the paper, calling out jobs.

'Construction consultant . . . insurance salesman . . . vacuum mechanic –'

'I bet that job sucks,' Brendan joked.

'. . . cat groomer . . . window washer . . . house cleaner . . . bond broker –'

'Aren't there any design jobs?' Ivy interrupted.

Camilla scanned the column. 'Here's one,' she said. 'Denture designer. What do you think that is?'

Brendan coughed. 'Hey, this reminds me of a joke,' he blurted. 'What's black and white and red all over?'

'A vampire having a midnight snack?' Camilla guessed innocently.

Olivia's heart skipped a beat, and she could swear that the three vamps around the table turned a shade whiter.

'I was going to say a newspaper,' Brendan mumbled weakly.

After a few more minutes, Olivia had to agree with her friends that there were no openings that seemed right for Mr Vega.

'So much for Plan C,' sighed Ivy as the bell for the end of lunch rang.

'Fortunately,' Olivia said, 'there are still twenty-three letters left in the alphabet.'

🦇　　　🦇　　　🦇

After school, Ivy leaned close to the science hall bathroom mirror and carefully applied Olivia's shimmery eye shadow. At the next sink, her sister scrunched up her face and sprayed herself with a can of Pale Beauty spray-on whitener.

Ivy shifted from one sneaker-clad foot to the other and wriggled herself around in Olivia's stone-washed jeans. They were going to have to spend the whole night as each other, because by the time *Wicked* was over, it would be too late to get away and switch back.

'You know this is going to be our trickiest switch yet,' said Olivia as she reached for Ivy's thick eyeliner. 'We have to fool our parents for hours.'

I don't know if I can be perky for that long, Ivy thought. 'What if we get caught?' she said.

'Think of it this way,' Olivia said, blinking dramatically at herself with her freshly blackened eyes. 'If you get grounded for a month, you can't leave the house to go to Europe.'

'There are some things you'll need to know if you're going to convince my dad you're me,' said

Ivy. In the mirror, she practised smiling so her teeth showed. 'Like what?' said Olivia.

'Things that might be hard for you to, um, *digest*,' said Ivy. She watched her sister's reflection for a reaction, but Olivia didn't notice her choice of words.

'Trust me, nothing could be worse than flying monkeys,' said Olivia. She flattened her lips to apply Ivy's deep plum lipstick.

'Good,' said Ivy. She turned and flashed her sister her best Olivia-like smile. 'Then you'll be happy to know Marshmallow Platelets is your favourite cereal.'

'Oh, gross!' Olivia cried.

An hour later, Ivy did her best to skip up to the front door of the Abbott's split-level home. Even after Olivia's in-depth briefing on life in her house, she couldn't keep from being a little nervous. *Stick a bat in a bunny hole*, she thought, and sooner or later it's going to flap its wings. Still, she'd just have to do her best. It would all be worth it to see *Wicked* and help her sister.

Ivy swung her ponytail around, moistened her pink lips, smiled as brightly as she could, and rang the doorbell. Soon enough, the door swung open to reveal Olivia's mom, Audrey Abbott, wearing a dark blue skirt and pearls.

'Hi, Mom!' said Ivy.

'Hi, Olivia,' said Mrs Abbott. She craned her neck to look past Ivy into the street. 'Everything OK?'

'For sure,' Ivy chirped. 'Why?'

'Don't you have your house key?' Mrs Abbott asked.

I rang the doorbell to what's supposed to be my own house, Ivy thought, horrified. *There go my bat wings: flap, flap!*

Ivy smacked her forehead with the palm of her hand. 'I must have forgotten it,' she said. 'Sorry, Mom.'

'It's OK, honey,' Mrs Abbott said. 'You'd better go upstairs and change, though. We're leaving for the show in half an hour.'

Luckily, Ivy made it to the theatre and into her seat without saying anything else that might give her away. The first act of *Wicked* was killer. When the lights rose for intermission, Ivy couldn't take her eyes off the stage. The performances, the music, the story – everything was seriously spectacular. The name of the wicked witch echoed in her head.

'Elphaba . . . Elphaba . . . Elphaba! Olivia!' Mrs Abbott was shaking her arm. 'Olivia, are you OK, honey?'

'This show sucks,' Ivy whispered in awe.

Mrs Abbott's face fell. 'You hate it?'

All at once Ivy remembered that she was supposed to be her sister. *Flap, flap!*

'I mean,' she scrambled, 'it sucks in a *good* way. It's slang. I totally love the show!'

'You do?' Mrs Abbott looked surprised.

Not too enthusiastic, you dingbat! Ivy thought to herself. *This is supposed to be Olivia's therapy!*

'What I'm trying to say,' she looked at Olivia's mom sincerely, 'is that it's really helping.'

'Oh, sweetie!' Mrs Abbott threw her arms around her and hugged her close. 'I'm so happy to hear that.' She pulled back slightly and patted Ivy's cheek. 'Let's go get you a Diet Coke.'

Ivy followed Olivia's mother up the aisle and out to the lobby. *It's awfully nice having a mom,* she thought to herself.

As they stood in line for the concession stand, everyone was buzzing excitedly about how great the show was. Ivy was trying to eavesdrop on the conversation the people in front of her were having about the costumes when she overheard someone say, 'We've finally secured the funds for the largest art exhibit in the history of the museum!'

Ivy recognised Walter Grosvenor, the curator of the Franklin Grove Art Museum, standing at the bar. She'd know him anywhere, because he had that classic vamp hairstyle with grey hair on the sides and slick, pitch-black hair on top. He picked up his drink and pressed through the crowd, followed by an enormous man in a fancy dark suit and an enormous floppy red bow tie.

'Oh?' the heavy man said. 'What will the exhibit be?'

'A permanent installation dedicated to the history of Franklin Grove,' Mr Grosvenor said as he walked by Ivy. 'All we need is a long-standing member of the community to design it and serve as its permanent curator.' He rested his drink on the ledge of a pillar.

My dad would bite his own neck to design an exhibit at the Franklin Grove Art Museum! Ivy thought. She tried to hear more, but Audrey was talking.

'I'll never forget the night you saw *The Wizard of Oz* on TV,' Mrs Abbott said. 'You loved it at first.'

Ivy nodded her head automatically, inching closer to Mr Grosvenor. He was saying something about 'someone with a passion for the arts and a deep appreciation for the diversity of Franklin Grove'.

'But then that woman with the crooked nose came on and said, "I'll get you my pretty!"' Audrey said. They crept forward in line, and Mr Grosvenor fell out of range. Ivy tapped her toe nervously, desperate to hear more. Finally it was their turn, and the moment the bartender handed Ivy her Diet Coke, she said, 'Let's go stand over there,' gesturing toward the post where Mr Grosvenor was standing with his friend.

Audrey followed her gaze. 'Brian Warchuck!' she gasped. 'Why didn't you say you saw him! My, he's grown.'

'Huh?' said Ivy. Then she saw that, standing directly on the opposite side of the pillar from Mr Grosvenor was a lanky, pimply teenaged boy in a skinny tie.

Olivia's mom grabbed her hand and plunged through the crowd. 'Brian!' she called. 'You remember my daughter, Olivia, Olivia Abbott?'

Brian Warchuck turned a brighter shade of red than Ivy thought possible, even for a human. 'Olivia Abbott?' he squeaked.

'Hi,' Ivy said tentatively. She angled her head towards the pillar. From what she could tell, Mr

Grosvenor was now talking about German Expressionism.

'Olivia still talks about you!' Mrs Abbott said.

'I do?' Ivy responded.

'You do?' Brian gawked. A bead of sweat emerged in the middle of his forehead.

'One never forgets one's first love,' Mrs Abbott said wistfully. 'Even if it happened in kindergarten.'

No way! Ivy thought. Brian Warchuck stared at her with a dreamy, toothy grin. His hair was plastered to his head, and he had exactly three reddish whiskers protruding from his chin.

'So what brings you to Franklin Grove, Brian?' Mrs Abbott asked. 'We've only lived here since September.'

'We moved to Creemore a few years ago,' Brian stammered, unable to take his eyes off Ivy. 'It's only two towns over.' His Adam's apple bobbed nervously. 'I still have your blue blankie, Olivia. Do you still have my fuzzy bear?'

'I don't think so,' Ivy shook her head.

'You threw Fuzzy out?' Brian's lip trembled. 'But you said you would never abandon Fuzzy!'

Flap, flap! Ivy thought, and her mouth went bone dry. What if Brian was on to her? She looked at Olivia's mom's desperately.

'Of course you have that teddy bear, honey,' Mrs Abbott said. 'It's on the shelf in your room.'

Ivy almost collapsed with relief. 'Oh, *that* bear,' she croaked gratefully. 'Of course.'

The lights in the lobby flashed on and off, signalling everyone to return to their seats for the second act.

'Oh, well. Time to go back in. Bye!' Ivy said desperately.

'I can take a bus to see you some time,' Brian offered.

'You should probably call first,' Ivy said quickly before tugging Mrs Abbott towards the doors to the auditorium. *I have got to talk to Olivia about her taste in boys*, she thought.

'We're in the white pages under "Abbott"!' Olivia's mom called over her shoulder.

As they took their seats, Ivy's mind returned to Mr Grosvenor, the opening at the Art Museum, and her friends' plan to keep her dad in Franklin Grove.

He's the perfect candidate for that museum job, she thought. *But he'd never put himself up for consideration.*

'You should have given Brian your e-mail address,' Audrey whispered in her ear as the actors took the stage.

That's it! thought Ivy. *I'll send the museum curator an e-mail on behalf of my dad!*

'Good thinking,' Ivy whispered back. 'Thanks, Mom!'

🦇   🦇   🦇

Olivia carefully folded a pair of black cargo shorts and put them atop the other clothes in a cardboard box. She grabbed the tape gun off Ivy's bed and sealed the box shut. Then she took a black magic marker and wrote on the side: 'IVY'S SUMMER CLOTHES'.

She collapsed on the bed. *Ouch!* She reached underneath herself and pulled out one of Ivy's huge black purses, brimming with cosmetics and school supplies. *At least if Ivy has to move,* she thought sadly, *she'll have a few boxes that are neatly packed.*

Olivia had been half-relieved, half-disappointed when she got to Ivy's house and found a note from Mr Vega saying he'd be home late. On the one hand, she didn't have to worry about keeping up her Ivy act. But on the other, she'd been quite excited about spending some time with her father. She wanted to show him what he'd be missing if he moved – how nice and smart and cool she was – even if he did think she was actually Ivy.

At that moment, Olivia heard a noise from upstairs. 'Ivy!' Mr Vega's voice called. 'I need your help!'

Olivia sprang to her feet and bounded to the mirror on the inside of one of Ivy's wardrobe doors. She shook her body to get her perk out, and brushed her hair down in front of her face with her hands.

'Coming,' she called. All of a sudden, she felt totally nervous. *What if he sees through the switch?* she thought.

She speed-trudged upstairs to the foyer, bracing herself for the moment Mr Vega first saw her dressed as Ivy. But when she got there, her father had his back to her, his heels dug into the stone floor. In the dim light, he was trying to pull what looked like an enormous grey furry beast through the front door by its tiny head.

'Help . . . me,' he groaned.

'What is that thing?' Olivia squealed, immediately kicking herself because her sister would never be so excitable.

'The Christmas tree,' her dad gasped. 'It's stuck!'

Sure enough, Olivia could see that her father wasn't grabbing monster fur at all – he was holding the branches of an enormous tree. Strangely, the leaves were silvery grey instead of green.

Her father grunted with effort. Olivia ran up to where the tree met the doorway, but there wasn't any place for her to grab on. She bent down and saw that there was a small space between the tree and the doorjamb.

'Hurry!' her father called hoarsely.

Olivia scooted underneath on all fours and emerged outside, where the chill of the air immediately pricked her skin. She hurried to the bottom of the tree and pushed on its cut trunk. Nothing budged. She tried again. Nothing.

'P-O-W,' she cheered quietly to herself as she leaned into the tree with all her might, 'E and R! That's how you get the Pow-er!'

All at once, the tree slipped through the door like a giant pipe cleaner. Inside, there was a terrible crash. Olivia rushed in.

Her father was splayed on the floor, the tip of the tree in his lap. He was laughing. Olivia couldn't remember if she'd ever heard him laugh like that before.

'Now that is the way to bring in the Christmas spirit!' he said giddily.

'Are you OK?' Olivia asked.

'Now I am,' he said. 'Thank you, Ivy. You always were strong and clever.'

'Thanks,' said Olivia softly. It felt good to hear him compliment her, even if he didn't know it was her.

'I had wanted to surprise you,' Mr Vega admitted. He reached into the back pocket of his pants and handed Olivia a folded piece of paper. She unfolded it with trembling fingers.

It was the charcoal drawing he'd been working on a few days ago, when Olivia and her sister had interrupted him in his study. She could see now that it was a design for the most amazing Christmas tree ever.

'It's a Silver Ash,' her father told her. 'I ordered it specially.'

In the drawing, the Christmas tree looked almost as enormous as it was in real life, reaching from floor to ceiling of the foyer. The whole thing was so elaborately decorated that it looked covered in a delicate spider web of sparkling ornaments. At the top was the silhouette of a bat.

'It's beautiful,' Olivia whispered.

'I wanted to do something special for you,' her father smiled gently, 'to celebrate our last Christmas in this house.'

'Thanks . . . Dad. I love it,' Olivia said genuinely. Then he reached over and gave her a big hug, and Olivia's heart almost burst.

'Can we decorate it tonight?' she asked after a second.

He shook his head. 'Not tonight, darling. It's too late. We'll do it tomorrow.'

'Sure,' Olivia said softly, trying to keep the disappointment out of her voice.

A little while later, Olivia lay in the dark on top of her sister's coffin, replaying the moment when her father had hugged her in her mind. She smiled to herself. *Maybe Ivy will agree to switch again tomorrow*, she thought as she drifted off to sleep. *Maybe my father and I can decorate the tree together.*

Chapter Six

Ten minutes before her social studies exam, first thing on Friday morning, Olivia was huddled in a stall in the science hallway bathroom, rushing to switch clothes with her sister. She frantically peeled Ivy's black leggings from her legs.

'You saw Brian Warchuck?' she said to the metal divider.

'He's still in love with you,' Ivy's voice echoed from the next stall.

Olivia's heart raced. 'How'd he look?' She'd been waiting her entire life to see her Prince Charming again!

'Like a pencil with pimples,' Ivy's voice answered matter-of-factly.

'Noooo,' said Olivia, grabbing the pink fuzzy sweater Ivy had just thrown over the divider. 'He used to be so cute!'

'Well, he still is, if you like boys who plaster their hair to their foreheads with Vaseline,' Ivy told her. Olivia heard her sister's stall door open and shut. 'Anyway, you'd better hurry up. We're going to be late for our last midterm, and I still haven't told you about how my dad's not moving to Europe.'

'What did you say?' Olivia gasped. She threw open her stall door to see her sister grinning at her with her arms crossed.

'We're not moving,' Ivy said. 'My father's dream job has come up – and it's right here in Franklin Grove!'

Olivia listened intently as her sister told her

all about overhearing the vamp curator's conversation about the job opening at the art museum. It sounded *perfect*!

'Do you really think he'd put himself up for it?' Olivia asked.

'He already has,' Ivy said, raising one eyebrow. 'I sent Mr Grosvenor an email from my web account using your parents' computer last night. I talked all about my qualifications: my long-time patronage of the museum, what an upstanding member of the community I am, all the design awards I've won. It was some of my best writing.'

'I didn't know you'd got design awards,' Olivia said, impressed.

'The email wasn't from *me*,' explained Ivy. 'It was from Charles Vega. Since my email address is just my last name, Mr Grosvenor will never know the difference.'

'You forged an email?' asked Olivia.

'Desperate times call for desperate measures,' Ivy stated. 'Even jail would be better than Europe.'

That's true, Olivia thought. 'I'd bring you cupcakes,' she said. 'And we could talk on the phone through plexiglass, like they do in the movies.'

A few moments later, they were back to looking like themselves, and Olivia and her sister were speeding down the hall toward social studies.

'Can I ask you a favour?' Olivia asked, remembering the previous night with her father.

'Anything,' Ivy said. 'As long as I don't have to go to cheerleading practice.'

Olivia lowered her voice as they made their way through the bustling crowds. 'Can we switch again tonight?'

'Two nights in a row?' replied Ivy. 'My skin will start turning pink!'

Olivia smiled. 'Our dad's always so weird around me because I'm human. But when I pretend to be you, he's more relaxed. It's the only time I ever get to see what he's really like. He wants to decorate the Christmas tree tonight.'

Ivy rolled her eyes. 'That'll take *hours*.'

'It would really mean a lot to me,' Olivia said softly.

They stopped outside the door to social studies. 'Sure,' Ivy agreed. 'It wouldn't be such a stake in the heart to spend some more time at your house. I'm starting to feel like Audrey Abbott's my mom, too.'

'Thanks, Ivy,' Olivia said gratefully. 'It might be my last chance to spend time with him.'

'Not if I can help it!' Ivy said firmly.

Olivia smiled at her sister's determination, and then followed her into the classroom to take their social studies exam.

At the end of the day, Ivy sat shivering on the school steps, waiting for Olivia's mom to pick her up. She wiggled her toes in Olivia's blue suede boots to keep them warm. Occasionally, someone would walk down the steps past her and say, 'Have a good break, Olivia.'

'Bye,' Ivy replied sadly.

She had been so focused on studying for exams and trying to convince her dad not to move that the final day of school had crept up on her. It wasn't until she'd sat down on the steps that it had really hit her that these might be her final moments at Franklin Grove Middle School.

What if the job with the museum doesn't work out? she thought. She'd checked her email in the library right before she came outside, and there was still no response from Mr Grosvenor.

Ivy looked over her shoulder at the majestic silhouette of the school against the grey afternoon sky. She and her father had moved to Franklin Grove when she was still a baby. She'd never known anywhere else. *No boarding school in Luxembourg could ever compete with this place*, she thought.

Faces paraded through her mind. Olivia, pink and perky, in the hallway on the day they met; Brendan, drop-dead gorgeous against the lockers, asking her out for the first time; Sophia, bounding up with her camera to call another emergency bathroom meeting.

In five days, she was supposed to leave almost all the people who meant the most to her: her best friend, her sister, her boyfriend. She felt like her grave was about to be dug up, taking her away from the place where she wanted to spend eternity.

Suddenly, Ivy felt her eyes welling up. *Don't wallow,* she commanded herself. *If you start crying, your spray-on tan will run. Besides, you still have five days. All is not lost!*

Olivia's mom's car appeared at the curb. Ivy quickly composed herself, grabbed Olivia's bag, and bounced down the steps.

When she got in the car, Ivy could tell Mrs Abbott was still over the moon about the miraculous affect *Wicked* had had on her daughter. Music from the show was playing on the car's CD player. 'I know how much you loved it,' Audrey said, 'so I ran out and bought you the soundtrack!'

Her enthusiasm was infectious, and pretty soon Ivy was singing along with Olivia's mom at the top of her lungs. *Sophia and Brendan would die if they saw me belting out show tunes!* she thought.

When they got home, Olivia's mom headed

for the kitchen. 'Your father and I are just doing some découpage,' she said. 'I'll call you when dinner's ready.'

'What's découpage?' Ivy risked.

'You know,' Audrey said. 'It's when you make a collage on a vase or something, and then you paint it over with glue. I know it's your least favourite craft.' Audrey started to walk away, and Ivy's heart sank.

'Can I do one?' she asked tentatively.

Audrey smiled. 'Of course! I just didn't think you'd be interested.'

Ivy shrugged, and before she knew it she was engrossed in decorating her own vase, using cut-outs from a garden magazine. She'd succeeded in ringing the base with bright green grass, above which danced a circle of ladybugs. Now she was working on a band of tiny golden buttercups.

'That's lovely, honey!' Audrey encouraged.

'Thanks,' said Ivy, carefully pasting on another flower. 'I'm going to give it to Ol– I mean Ivy for Christmas,' she corrected herself hurriedly. 'She'll totally love it,' she added, swinging her ponytail enthusiastically.

Mr Abbott looked up from his ceremonial wooden sword stand, which he was decorating with cut-outs of Bruce Lee doing different kung fu moves. 'What a great idea,' he said. 'She can take it with her to Europe.'

Ivy felt the wind go out of her, and Olivia's mother and father shared a concerned look.

'We know how hard Ivy going must be for you, Olivia,' Audrey said gently.

Ivy stared silently at the yellow flower on her finger for a long moment. 'It's the hardest thing I've ever had to face,' she admitted quietly. Then, with a deep breath, she carefully affixed the flower to Olivia's vase.

On an upper rung of the ladder, Olivia balanced on the steel toes of Ivy's boots. She had to stretch to attach the final blood-red rose to the loose web of silver wires that she and her father had arranged around the Christmas tree, according to his design. Out of the corner of her eye, she could see him down below, placing the last candles amid the branches.

They'd been decorating for nearly two hours, and Olivia had to admit that the finished tree was going to be even more breathtaking than she'd expected. Apart from the sparkling web of wires, the only other decorations were pale candles and red roses everywhere. It was the perfect mix of intricate design and simple ornamentation.

The only bad part was that she and her dad had barely spoken the whole time, apart from when he told her that they'd add the silver 'Christmas Bites' last of all. She didn't even know what Christmas Bites were.

Olivia kept trying to think of something to talk about. She couldn't talk about why Mr Vega was moving to Europe, or the fact that he was her father. Even complimenting the tree too enthusiastically seemed like a mistake, since she was supposed to be acting like her tight-lipped Goth sister who was still sort of mad at her dad. Anyway, Mr Vega seemed totally lost in his own thoughts.

'I think we are ready to hang the Christmas Bites,' her father announced suddenly, and disappeared into the kitchen to get them.

Descending the ladder, Olivia tried to imagine what Christmas Bites were. *Glow-in-the-dark fangs? Chunks of red meat?* Her father re-emerged with a small stack of notebook-sized boxes. *Candies made of human flesh?* She held her breath as he opened a box to reveal a bunch of foil-wrapped chocolates, each one shaped like a small bowling pin.

They're almost like Hershey's kisses, Olivia thought, relaxing.

Her father handed some Bites to her, and he took some himself. As Olivia started to hang them among the sweet-smelling roses, she noticed that each one was decorated like a different profession. There was a tiny-headed baker, with a poofy white hat. And a tiny doctor, with a stethoscope hanging down on to his round belly. And one bearded guy with a shovel, who Olivia guessed was a gravedigger.

These are hilarious! Olivia chuckled to herself.

'You always found the tradition of Christmas Bites amusing,' her father's voice suddenly intoned, almost to himself. 'When you were very small, you used to have tea parties with them. You were very particular. The teacher had to sit next to the construction worker and so on. And then, just when your tiny guests were getting comfortable, then came your favourite part of all.'

His face bloomed into a smile. 'You would bite off all their heads.' He nodded nostalgically to himself. 'How you would laugh when their blood spurted.'

Olivia looked at the Bites in her hand. *These have blood in them!* she thought queasily.

After a moment's pause, Mr Vega focused his eyes on Olivia's, and his smile dissolved. 'This last while, as we have been decorating,' he said in a pained voice, 'I have been trying to figure out how to say I am sorry to you, Ivy.'

'For what?' Olivia quavered.

'For taking you away from here. From this house, from your friends, from . . .' His voice trailed off, and he shook his head. 'I do not want to leave here either. This town, it gave me a home when I had none. This community gave me a life when I thought mine was over. I do not think there is another place like Franklin Grove in the world.'

'Then why are you going?' Olivia asked.

Something dark and hard flashed across her father's eyes. 'I could not live with myself if I did not know in the darkest crypts of my soul that leaving is the best thing for us,' he said firmly. 'Sometimes, change is for the best.'

This might be the only chance I ever have to try to talk him out of it, thought Olivia. 'I've already been through quite a lot of change lately,' she tried. 'I just found a twin sister I never knew I had. Besides, I've got great friends here, I'm on the school paper and . . . and . . . I just started dating this really cool guy . . .'

'I know, sweetheart,' Mr Vega said.

'Anyway, I bet there are lots of great new job opportunities for you right here in Franklin Grove,' Olivia went on.

Her father nodded distractedly, but to Olivia's disappointment, he didn't respond. After a moment, he lifted his chin towards her and cleared his throat. 'Tell me about Olivia. How is she doing in school?'

Olivia was caught completely off guard. She'd never thought her father was at all interested in her. 'Um,' she began. 'I think she does well. I think she might get straight As on her report card – as long as everything went OK with her algebra exam.'

Her father smiled. 'Good,' he said. 'That's good. And does she have many friends?'

'Well, you know,' Olivia said, picking up steam, 'she only just moved to Franklin Grove in

September, so she's still getting to know people.'
She thought of Camilla. 'She's really close to
Camilla Edmunson, this girl who's really smart
and into sci-fi books.'

Her father nodded approvingly.

'And she hangs out a lot with Sophia and
Brendan,' she added. 'But I'm, like, totally her
best friend.' Olivia stopped herself. She was
getting confused talking about herself this way.
Plus I just sounded like a cheerleader instead of a Goth,
she thought, scanning her father's face to see if
he'd noticed.

'And Olivia's a really good cheerleader,' she
couldn't resist adding.

'She is a remarkable young person,' Mr Vega
said tenderly. 'I am sincerely glad we got to meet
and know her.'

Olivia felt like her father's compliment had
raised her into the air, so that she stood for a

moment, perfectly balanced and triumphant in his palm. *He accepts me*, she thought. *He cares about me and who I am. If he leaves, at least I know that.*

'I know how painful –' his voice became hoarse, like he was going to cry – 'it will be for you to leave her,' he said. He touched his eyes briefly. When he spoke again, his voice was steady. 'But moving to Europe is something that I have to do. I hope that one day, you can forgive me.' He reached into his pocket and held out what looked like a candy cane. 'A peace offering,' he said hopefully.

With a small, grateful smile, Olivia accepted his offering. Funnily enough, candy canes were her favourite. He reached his arm around her and gave her a hug. She closed her eyes and buried her face in his shoulder for a moment, trying to savour the feeling.

Then she began peeling the wrapper off the candy cane.

'Bloody canes have always been your favourite,' her father said.

Olivia's fingers froze. 'On second thoughts, I'll save it for later,' she gulped, slipping the candy into the pocket of Ivy's black jeans. 'Because it's such a special treat.'

After they'd hung the Christmas Bites, Olivia and her father squeezed in next to each other on the top wrung of the ladder. In his hands, he held a dark grey box. He opened it, and took out a sleek black velvet bat the size of an eagle.

'Our Holiday Bat,' he announced.

The bat's wings unfurled. Olivia took one wing in her hand, while her father held the other. And, together, they reached out and placed it at the top of the tree.

Chapter Seven

'That was delicious, Mom,' Ivy said, as she helped Mrs Abbott clear the table after dinner. Ivy didn't usually eat tofu steaks, but Olivia's mom had made them with a red wine reduction sauce that tasted surprisingly like blood.

'Thanks, honey,' Mrs Abbott said appreciatively. Just then, the doorbell rang. Mrs Abbott slipped off her apron and went to answer it.

Maybe that's Olivia, thought Ivy nervously. *What if Dad caught her trying to pass herself off as me?*

She heard Mrs Abbott open the front door, followed by a chorus of high-pitched noises – it sounded like a flock of monstrous giants birds from an old horror movie.

Ivy crept down the hall and poked her head around the corner. Two little human girls wearing tutus and tiaras were chasing each other around Mrs Abbott's legs, screaming their heads off. In the open doorway stood a woman who must have been their mother.

Ivy whipped her head back before anyone saw her. She swallowed hard. *Baby bunnies!* she thought.

'We really appreciate you and Olivia watching the girls,' the woman at the door was saying.

'Of course. Go and have a great time with Jeff,' Ivy overheard Mrs Abbott reply.

The kids are staying! Ivy realised. She would rather have been buried alive. Nothing could be more dangerous and strange than a tiny human, let alone two of them!

'Olivia!' Audrey called. 'Casey and Stacey are here!'

Ivy took a deep breath and forced herself to put one bobby-sock in front of the other. She made her way down the hall and stood frozen in the living-room doorway. In front of the fireplace, Olivia's father was wound up in a jump-rope, one little girl pulling on each end.

'Not so tight,' he said, 'or I'll have to use my Li Ching on you.' He tried to laugh, but he was clearly helpless.

'Here's Olivia,' Audrey said when she saw Ivy.

The girls dropped the jump rope handles and started leaping up and down. Their shrieking took on a new intensity. 'OLIIIIIVIAAAAAA! OLIIIIIVIAAAAAA!'

Audrey must have noticed the horrified expression on Ivy's face, because she said, 'We promised Carol, remember? We're taking care of the girls while she and Jeff go to dinner for their anniversary.'

I'm going to kill my sister, thought Ivy.

Casey and Stacey raced up to Ivy. She had no idea which was which, but one was wearing a yellow leotard and tutu, and the other was wearing a pink one. She forced herself not to recoil as they tugged at her hands.

'TEACH US A CHEER! A CHEER! A CHEER!' they shrieked.

'I don't know any cheers,' Ivy stammered.

Olivia's mother and father both stared at her.

'Just kidding,' Ivy smiled weakly.

'Well, then,' said Audrey. 'I'll just leave you to work your magic.' She winked at Ivy and walked out of the room.

Don't leave me! Ivy wanted to yell. She had zero experience with human kids. This wasn't going to be like hanging out with Brendan's little sister.

Playing 'Vampire Hunter' was not an option. *What am I supposed to do with a pair of hyper baby bunnies for a whole evening?* she thought frantically. She didn't know ballet, and she wasn't about to have a conversation about ponies.

'WHAT ARE YOU WAITING FOR, OLIVIA?' the girl in the yellow tutu screamed. *Human children are like animals,* Ivy thought. *They can smell fear.* She couldn't let on that she had no idea what to do.

'Look, Olivia,' the girl in the pink tutu said. 'We got dressed up for you.'

'You did?' said Ivy, and both little girls beamed up at her angelically. The one in the pink tutu was missing two front teeth. All at once, Ivy realised that these little bunnies were expecting her to be nothing more than the perky, peppy, fun Olivia they knew. *All I have to do is give them what they want,* she thought.

Ivy clasped her hands together. 'Well. Those are like the prettiest, sparkliest, most princess-y outfits ever!' she said, giving her best Olivia-ponytail-flip. 'I totally *love* them!'

'I told you she'd be impressed,' the girl in the yellow tutu said, beaming at her sister.

❤   ❤   ❤

Olivia was sitting at the table in Ivy's kitchen as her father checked the oven.

'What's for dinner?' she asked, her leg bouncing nervously under the table.

'It is a surprise,' he answered mysteriously.

This afternoon, Olivia and Ivy had agreed that she'd make up some excuse at dinner time so she wouldn't have to eat anything that would make her puke. 'Just say "I'm not feeling well" or "I'm trying a new diet",' Ivy had said.

But now the evening had been going so well that Olivia didn't want to spoil it. Her father had set the table for them really nicely. 'Can you give me a hint?' she asked anxiously.

Her father came over and lit a candle in the centre of the table. 'In honour of our move,' he said proudly, 'I have made a European dish that is renowned for its taste, texture and iron content.'

Olivia's stomach churned. *That means something bloody, I know it,* she thought. She gulped her glass of water. 'I don't think I'm hungry,' she said after a moment.

Her father's face fell, and Olivia felt super-guilty. 'Won't you even try a bite?' her dad pleaded. 'It's quite a delicacy. In fact, it's part of a traditional human breakfast.'

It can't be too gross then, Olivia thought. *OK, I'll try it.*

Her father slipped on a grey oven mitt and crossed the kitchen to pull something out of the oven. She could tell he was slicing something. He returned and set a plate before her. It had two thick patties on it that looked like dirt.

Olivia poked one with a fork. 'What is it?'

'Black pudding,' her father said proudly. 'It's very popular in England.'

That doesn't sound so bad, Olivia thought. 'What's in it?'

'It's congealed blood sausage, cut into slices,' her father said matter-of-factly.

'*Humans* eat that?' Olivia blurted.

'All the time,' her dad replied, sitting down across from her with his own plate. He cut a huge piece and popped it in his mouth. He shut his eyes blissfully, savouring the taste. 'Mmmmm.' He gestured towards Olivia's plate encouragingly, but she couldn't move. She was too busy concentrating on not breathing through her nose.

'Go on,' he nodded.

Olivia's fork and knife shook in her hands. She

forced herself to cut a piece the size of her pinky fingernail. She adjusted her glass of water so the moment she took a bite she could chug.

'Don't let it get cold,' her father directed.

Olivia felt like the whole Franklin Grove cheerleading squad was doing handsprings in her stomach. *You have no choice*, she told herself. *You have to eat it!* She shut her eyes as tight as she could and raised the trembling fork to her mouth.

Ivy tilted the living-room lamp so that it shone on Casey and Stacey like a spotlight. Olivia's mom and the girls' own mother, who'd arrived to pick them up, watched from the couch. Instead of teaching the girls a dance or a cheer, Ivy had helped them write a little play, and now was their big performance.

'And so Princess Casey and Ballerina Stacey were trapped by the evil wizard,' Ivy narrated.

She swung the lamp towards Ivy's father, who was sitting in the corner in an easy chair, rubbing his hands together. 'The infamous Accountant-O!' she announced. Mr Abbott laughed menacingly.

'Eeeeeeeeeeekkkkk!' shrieked the girls.

'Isn't Steve frightening?' Audrey whispered happily to her friend, who nodded.

'They waited for their princes to rescue them,' Ivy continued.

'My prince will rescue us,' said Casey, ruffling her yellow tutu nervously with her fingers. 'He has twenty-three racing cars, plus he's a veterinarian.'

Stacey stepped forward. 'My prince will save us,' she enunciated, 'because he's really rich and he has a moustache.'

The moms giggled.

'They waited and waited,' said Ivy. 'Accountant-

O's dungeon was really gross.' She reached into a plastic bag full of props. 'There were worms.' She reached out a hand and showered the girls with cut-up pieces of string.

'Eeeewwwwww!' they freaked.

'And there was a monster chained to the wall in the corner,' Ivy added. She gave a huge roar, and the girls ran around screaming. Ivy reached into her prop bag and pulled out a spray bottle. She sprayed the girls with mist. 'It sneezed on them.'

'Yuck!' the girls yelled, shielding their eyes.

'But still their princes did not come,' Ivy intoned. Casey and Stacey pouted dramatically. From the shadows, Mr Abbott laughed evilly again.

'Princess Casey and Ballerina Stacey grew impatient,' Ivy said.

Stacey reached into an imaginary pocket in her pink tutu and pulled out an imaginary cell phone. 'Where are you?' she said. 'You were supposed to be here hours ago!' She listened like a real actress, and then hung up. 'I don't know what his problem is,' she huffed.

Casey crossed her arms. 'Boys!' she exclaimed. 'They're so unreliable.'

'Finally,' narrated Ivy, 'Princess Casey and Ballerina Stacey decided not to wait around any longer.'

'Let's get out of here,' Casey said to Stacey.

'They snuck up on the evil wizard, Accountant-O,' Ivy went on, following the girls with the lamp as they tiptoed up to Mr Abbott, who was punching things into an imaginary calculator and muttering numbers triumphantly.

Casey tapped him on the shoulder.

'What the?' Mr Abbott spun around in mock surprise and leapt to his feet.

Stacey balanced on one foot and raised her hands over her head, howling like a kung-fu master about to execute a killer move.

Mr Abbott's eyes widened. While he was distracted, Casey ran up and stamped on his foot.

'Ouch!' he cried. Ivy winced. They hadn't rehearsed that part.

Stacey karate-chopped him in the back.

'Ooh!' Mr Abbott said.

'You meanie!' Casey said and kicked him in the shin.

Doubled over, Mr Abbott craned his neck and shot Ivy a desperate look. 'Happily ever after!' he whispered. 'Happily ever –'

Both girls leapt on his back and the three of them collapsed on the living-room carpet with a crash.

'Uh, then Princess Casey and Ballerina Stacey ran away,' Ivy said quickly.

The girls sprang off Mr Abbott and dashed out of the room.

'And they lived happily ever after as best friends forever!' Ivy concluded.

The moms leapt up from the couch, cheering wildly. Casey and Stacey skipped back into the living room and curtsied to their audience daintily.

'Bravo! Bravo!' Audrey called. 'You take a bow too, Steve!'

'I can't,' Steve groaned from the floor. 'My back,' he said apologetically.

Ivy helped him to his feet and settled him into the easy chair. Then the girls came over, took her hands, and dragged her back in front of the couch. Ivy bowed with a flourish, her ponytail whipping forward.

I'm getting almost as good at being Olivia as Olivia! Ivy thought proudly. *I wonder how she's doing being me right now.*

🦇　　　🦇　　　🦇

I will never switch with Ivy during a mealtime again, Olivia thought. Her fork was still poised before her lips, with the same tiny chunk of black pudding on it. She kept trying to psyche herself up into putting the stuff into her mouth. *Mr Vega's going to get suspicious*, she thought desperately. *I'll have to do it now.* Suddenly, the phone rang in the next room.

'I'll get it,' her father said, dropping his napkin and rising from the table. She waited for him to leave the room before leaping from her chair. Then she rushed to the bin and scraped her two black pudding hockey pucks into the garbage with her fork, burying them under some crumpled paper towels. She'd just gotten back to her chair when Mr Vega re-entered the room.

'Who was it?' she asked, trying to sound nonchalant.

'A telemarketer,' her father grimaced as he

took his seat. 'He refused to take no for an answer. I kept telling him we do not use coffin wax.' He noticed Olivia's bare plate. 'You've already finished?'

'It was delicious,' Olivia gulped.

'I knew you'd like it,' her father said. 'I'll get you another helping.'

'No!' Olivia blurted. 'I mean, no, thank you.' She patted her belly like she was full. 'But thank you for going to all the trouble of making it for me.' She smiled and her father smiled back.

Chapter Eight

Early Saturday morning, Ivy quietly slid open the basement window at the back of her house, climbed inside, and crept down the stairs to her room.

Olivia was curled up on top of her bed, wearing Ivy's pyjamas with the gravestones on them and hugging a black cat pillow.

Only four days until Dad and I move, Ivy thought sadly as she looked down at her sleeping sister. *And then who knows when I'll see Olivia again?*

She decided to let her sister sleep for a few more minutes. She slipped into the chair in front of her desk and powered up the new laptop computer her dad had gotten her for boarding school. Ivy waited anxiously for her new emails to appear on the screen. Her heart sank when they finally did; there was still no response from the art museum. She let out a colossal sigh.

'Still nothing?' her sister's voice came from behind her.

Ivy wheeled her chair around to find Olivia sitting up in bed. 'We're running out of time,' Ivy told her.

Olivia nodded sadly and tightened her clutch on the black cat pillow.

'I know my father wouldn't turn down this job,' Ivy said. 'But we can't afford to sit around any more waiting for them to offer it to him.'

'Maybe we should take Sophia's advice,' said Olivia, rubbing the sleep from her eyes, 'except instead of chaining ourselves to your dad's car, we should chain ourselves to the front doors of the museum.'

That gave Ivy an idea. She spun her chair back around and went to the museum's website. 'They open at 10am on Saturdays,' she told her sister.

'I wasn't being serious,' Olivia told her.

'But I am,' Ivy said. 'We have to go down there and get them to offer Dad the job. Today.'

'In that case —' Olivia stretched her arms — 'we'd better call for back up.'

That afternoon, huddled in their own warm clothes on the sidewalk in front of the sleek, slanted marble façade of the Franklin Grove Art Museum, Ivy and her sister waited for Brendan to arrive. Ivy had called Sophia and Camilla to see if they could come too, but they each had plans. Ivy made a mental note to find time to get the whole group together in the next couple of days — it might be her last chance. She felt like a vampire in one of those old movies: there were only a few precious minutes until sunrise, and after that she'd turn to dust.

Brendan appeared down the block, wearing his heavy black parka, and just the sight of him made Ivy feel a little better. She waved and he picked up the pace. He came up and wrapped his arms around her, dipped her like they were ballroom dancing, and kissed her on the neck.

'Save it for the graveyard,' Olivia deadpanned beside them, and they both laughed. Then the three of them made their way across the slate courtyard and into the museum.

Ivy hadn't been there since her sixth-grade field trip, and she'd forgotten what an amazing place it was. The interior of the building was like the inside of a huge cone. An enormous ramp dotted with sculptures spiralled its way up the wall. Ivy stood with Brendan and Olivia in the centre of the grey marble floor on the ground level, and they could see people admiring art, snaking all the way up to the skylight and observation deck in the centre of the ceiling far above, like the hole in the top of a traffic cone.

Olivia went over to look at a glowing map of the building. 'The curator's office is on level four,' she said, and they started to make their way up the ramp.

Ivy couldn't help slowing down to look at some of the art. There was a life-sized sculpture of a sky diver made entirely of wire, and a tree that looked utterly real, except it had tiny peepholes carved in its trunk. When Ivy looked through one, she saw a completely realistic 3D highway running vertically, like a vein in the tree, with dozens of cars racing upward. Olivia was next to her, looking in another hole. 'Cool,' Olivia said. 'It's an art class drawing a model.'

Every peephole showed something different.

On level two, they passed an enormous papier-mâché zebra-like creature with rainbow stripes, huge blood-shot eyes, and the legs of a centipede.

Olivia wrinkled her nose. 'This one's weird.'

'It's hideous,' Ivy agreed.

Brendan bent over the little plaque alongside the sculpture. '"Zebraguts",' he read. '"Sculpture by Alice Bantam".'

Ivy's mouth dropped open. 'It's one of Alice's!'

'Can you imagine if your dad had fallen for her and you had to live with something like this?' Olivia giggled.

'No,' Ivy answered. 'Thank darkness that plan failed!'

Following the signs to the curator's office on the fourth level, they proceeded down a narrow hallway that shot off from the main ramp. At the end of it was a frosted door with Mr Grosvenor's name on it in gilded letters. Ivy knocked, and a moment later Mr Grosvenor himself pulled open the door. He was dressed in grey slacks and a white button-down shirt. 'Can I help you?'

Ivy tried to speak, but she was so nervous nothing came out of her mouth.

'We're here about the curator job for the new exhibit,' Olivia explained, stepping forward.

'Oh,' Mr Grosvenor said, looking the three of them up and down. 'I'm sure you're all very talented. But I'm afraid we're looking for someone with a bit more experience.'

'It's not for us,' said Brendan, glancing at Ivy encouragingly.

'I'm Ivy Vega,' Ivy croaked at last.

Mr Grosvenor's face lit up. 'Charles's daughter!' He extended his hand. 'Of course, I should have recognised you. I just read your father's email!' Ivy's heart quickened. 'And this must be the twin sister I've read about in the papers,' Mr Grosvenor went on.

Olivia shook the curator's hand as Brendan introduced himself, too.

'Welcome,' said Mr Grosvenor. 'Please, come in.'

Mr Grosvenor offered Ivy, Olivia and Brendan white plastic moulded chairs opposite his desk, which was completely bare except for a pad of paper and a bust of an old man's head made entirely of paperclips.

'So, what brings you to see me?' Mr Grosvenor asked, perching casually on the edge of the desk.

All day, Ivy had been mentally rehearsing a speech about how her father was the perfect person to set up the exhibition. 'Mr Grosvenor,' she began, 'I believe my father is ideally suited to the opening you are trying to fill. He is –'

'I agree completely,' Mr Grosvenor interrupted.

'Completely?' Ivy repeated in shock.

'I can't think of a stronger candidate,' Mr Grosvenor smiled. 'I'll be calling your father as soon as I have approval from the board.'

'When will that be?' asked Olivia quickly.

'Some time in January,' Mr Grosvenor replied. 'Or possibly February.'

Ivy's stomach dipped suddenly, like she was falling from a great height. 'Can't you do it sooner?' she pleaded.

'I wouldn't want to bother anyone before the new year,' Mr Grosvenor shrugged.

I should have known it wouldn't be so easy, Ivy thought.

Brendan nudged Ivy's boot with his own. He locked eyes with her, and she could tell he wanted her to tell the truth. Ivy looked towards Olivia, who also gave her a tiny nod.

'Is something wrong?' Mr Grosvenor enquired.

'Very,' Ivy admitted. Words started pouring out of her mouth. 'My dad didn't send you that email, Mr Grosvenor. I did. We're moving to Europe in four days. But I know that if my dad got this job in Franklin Grove, he'd stay. He's always wanted to work for the museum. You can't wait until the new year. By then, he'll be gone.' Ivy looked down at her lap. 'And so will I.'

'I see,' Mr Grosvenor said, sounding disappointed. With one hand, he stroked the streak of white hair on one side of his head.

'I should never have forged the email,' Ivy said, ashamed of herself. 'I know it was wrong. I'm sorry.'

Mr Grosvenor slowly went around to his chair and picked up the phone.

He's calling the police! Ivy thought in panic.

'Will you please remind me of your father's number?' Mr Grosvenor said instead. Ivy and Olivia both gasped. 'After all,' the curator smiled, 'we can't have Charles Vega leaving Franklin Grove without even *knowing* about this job.'

As Mr Grosvenor dialled, Ivy reached out on either side of her. Olivia grasped one hand and Brendan took the other. *This is our last chance,* she thought.

'Hello, Charles? Walter Grosvenor here. I'm sorry to ring you on a Saturday, but there is a once-in-a-lifetime opportunity here at the museum that I think you ought to consider seriously.'

Olivia, Brendan and Ivy sat on the edge of their seats as Mr Grosvenor described the position. Then he paused, listening to what Ivy's dad was saying on the other end.

'Of course, of course,' Mr Grosvenor said and

nodded at his three listeners encouragingly. Ivy squeezed the hands in hers excitedly.

But then Mr Grosvenor's face changed. 'Uh huh,' he said. He looked down at his desk, and jotted something on his pad of paper. 'Uh huh.' Brendan let go of Ivy's hand and put it on her shoulder. 'I understand,' said Mr Grosvenor quietly. 'Of course. Thank you.'

Mr Grosvenor gently hung up the phone. He shook his head. 'I'm sorry,' he said. 'Charles seemed genuinely interested, but he has firmly committed to this job in Europe. He said he wouldn't feel right changing his mind at this point.'

Ivy felt her whole body go limp. Olivia released Ivy's hand and covered her face.

'It appears we were too late after all,' Mr Grosvenor said, his voice full of disappointment.

All Ivy could think was, *It's over.*

'Thanks for your time, Mr Grosvenor,'

Brendan said after a moment. Then he led Ivy and her sister back out to the hallway and slowly down the long ramp. They spiralled down and down, farther and farther, and Ivy knew there was nothing she could to do to keep from hitting bottom.

🦇 🦇 🦇

As Olivia stood with her friends in the enormous stone courtyard in front of the museum, the frozen wind whipped her face. Her eyes began to water, but she couldn't tell whether it was from the cold or from the knowledge that she'd soon be losing both her sister and their father.

'He's not leaving because of the job,' she said softly. 'He's leaving because of me.'

Olivia expected Ivy to try to convince her that what she'd just said wasn't true. But when she looked into Ivy's eyes, she knew her sister had reached the same conclusion.

'He's determined to separate us,' Ivy admitted, 'just like he did when we were a year old.'

Olivia's cell phone rang. She stood there feeling hopeless for a long moment before answering it. 'Hello?'

'Hi, Olivia, it's Camilla. How'd it go at the museum?'

'Our dad got the job,' Olivia replied flatly. There was a squeal on the other end of the phone. 'And he turned it down,' she finished.

Across from her, Ivy and Brendan shared a hug.

'Oh, no,' Camilla's voice said softly. 'I'm so sorry.'

'Yeah,' Olivia shrugged. 'Me, too.'

'You sound like you could use some cheering up,' Camilla noted. 'Why don't we go bowling? I have a coupon for two free games. Ivy and Brendan can come, too.'

Olivia put her finger over the phone's

mouthpiece. 'Camilla wants us all to go bowling,' she told them.

'I don't feel like having fun,' Ivy said.

'Me neither,' Olivia agreed.

'Will you twins come on?' Brendan protested. 'Are you going to spend what might be your last few days together in Franklin Grove sulking and sighing? Or are you going to make the most of them?'

'I'm a professional sulker,' Ivy replied, smiling weakly.

'And I have a very dramatic sigh,' Olivia said, and sighed dramatically.

But Brendan wouldn't take no for an answer. 'You love bowling, Ivy. It's the only sport with an all-black ball. And you dig the shoes.' His dark eyes shone as he looked at Ivy entreatingly.

'OK,' Ivy conceded begrudgingly.

Why not? Olivia thought. She lifted the phone

back to her ear. 'Camilla? Prepare the gutters for our arrival.'

🦇   🦇   🦇

Brendan opened the door to the bowling alley, and the sounds of rolling balls and crashing pins poured out. Ivy's eyes adjusted to the indoor light, and across the alley she spotted Sophia standing beside Camilla, grinning hopefully and clutching her camera. In fact, the two of them were surrounded by people from school.

'SURPRISE!' the crowd cried, and a banner unfurled from the ceiling: 'WE'LL MISS YOU, IVY!'

The hairs on Ivy's neck stood on end. 'You didn't!' she cried across the bowling alley. Sophia's flash popped and the whole crowd broke out laughing and clapping.

'And to think we didn't even want to come!' Olivia whispered in awe beside her.

Sophia and Camilla ran up. 'Sophia told me how much you love bowling,' Camilla explained as she gave Ivy a hug, 'and my uncle owns the alley.'

'Camilla was like the funeral director of this whole thing,' Sophia admitted.

'I can't believe you two didn't tell me about this,' Olivia said, hugging Camilla. 'I could have helped!'

'We wanted to plan it all on our own,' Camilla answered proudly. 'Besides, you and Ivy have had other stuff going on, like Plans A through C.'

Camilla and Sophia led Ivy, Olivia and Brendan to the far side of the bowling alley, which Ivy could now see was cordoned off with a black velvet rope. Everyone was there: Toby Decker and the rest of the staff of the *Franklin Grove Scribe*, her math study group, the members of the planning committee for the All Hallows' Ball.

Miss Everling from the library came up and

squeezed Ivy's shoulder. 'So "your friend" is moving, huh?' she said. 'Well, there's no reason she can't come back to visit.' She stuck a grey pin to Ivy's long-sleeved black shirt. It read, 'Parlez-vous Anglais?'

A few minutes later, Ivy was chatting with Melissa, who'd been head of the All Hallows' Ball planning committee, when two loud *crack*s pierced the air. She turned to see Camilla standing in the middle of a bowling lane, holding a bowling pin in each hand. Sophia was beside her, holding something behind her back. Camilla cracked the pins together a third time, and the crowd quieted.

'Will our guest of honour please join us in lane nine?' Sophia called.

Ivy pressed through all of her friends. Brendan squeezed her hand briefly as she passed. She was about to cross the line into lane nine when Sophia shook her head. 'No, no, no,' she said playfully.

'No improper footwear in the lanes, please,' Camilla added.

Rolling her eyes, Ivy bent down, unlaced her boots, and shuffled on to the lane in her black socks.

'Anyone who knows Ivy,' Camilla said, raising her voice, 'knows about her distinctive sense of style. What would look ridiculous on the rest of us looks cool on her.'

'And there is one accessory,' continued Sophia, 'that she has always wanted.'

Camilla and Sophia both eyed Ivy's feet meaningfully. 'Bowling shoes!' they declared as one. Sophia produced a box from behind her back.

Ivy grabbed the box and tore off the lid. Inside were two black-and-white bowling shoes with smooth rust-coloured bottoms. *These are killer!* Ivy thought, immediately dropping them to the lane and slipping them on her feet. They were a perfect fit.

'Everyone chipped in,' Sophia told her.

Ivy looked out at the crowd of people smiling at her. 'Thank you all so –' But she couldn't continue. Tears began flowing down her cheeks.

Ivy looked up and glimpsed Garrick Stephens and the Beasts making their way through the crowd, but Garrick froze when he saw her bawling.

'We just wanted to say goodbye!' he protested. 'If we'd known it would make you feel so grim, we never would have crashed the party.'

Everybody laughed, including Ivy. *I bet there's no one like Garrick Stephens in Europe*, she thought.

'I'm even going to miss you Beasts,' Ivy said, smiling through her tears. Olivia crept on to the lane and handed her a Kleenex. Ivy wiped her eyes, and the tissue came away black with eye make-up.

'I'm so lucky,' Ivy said as loudly as she could, 'to have friends like all of you. I really, really don't want to move. But at least I'll be able to go, knowing that there are people here who love me.'

Sophia gave her a huge hug, and Camilla, Brendan and Olivia piled on.

'You'll always have friends in Franklin Grove,' Sophia said in her ear.

'You mean you guys aren't going to chain yourselves to my dad's car?' Ivy teased.

'We might,' Sophia smiled tearily.

Finally, the five of them separated and faced the crowd, their arms around each other.

'I'll never forget any of you,' Ivy promised. She wiped her eyes one more time and raised her arms in the air. 'Now, let's bowl!'

Chapter Nine

Olivia and Ivy sat together on a bench as the last guests milled around.

Toby Decker came up to say goodbye. 'Interested in writing a regular guest column for the *Scribe* about what it's like to be a Franklin Grover in Europe?' Toby asked with a grin.

Ivy's eyes opened wide. 'Are you serious?'

'You're the best writer we have,' Toby told her.

'That would be deadly,' Ivy said appreciatively. 'Thanks, Toby.'

'How cool is that?' Olivia remarked after Toby was gone. But Ivy didn't seem to hear

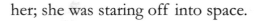

her; she was staring off into space.

'You OK?' Olivia nudged her sister.

'I was just thinking,' Ivy shrugged. 'I've been so caught up in trying to get Dad to change his mind that it never occurred to me to do anything like this for him. He's been in Franklin Grove for more than a decade. He should have a going-away party, too.'

'That's such a great idea,' Olivia exclaimed. 'Reminding him of all the people he'll miss could be just the thing to change his mind.'

'I doubt that,' Ivy admitted. 'But it would make him feel good. And maybe that's enough.'

Olivia nodded to herself. She had known Mr Vega – her father – for such a short time, it would be nice to do something for him before he disappeared from her life.

'What are you two whispering about?' Brendan leaned over the bench between them.

'We want to throw our dad a going-away party,' Ivy answered. 'Do you think it's too late?'

'Under normal circumstances, there wouldn't be enough time,' Brendan admitted. He waved to Camilla and Sophia to join them. 'But the good news,' he said as they trotted up, 'is that you have Operation FANGED at your disposal!'

🦇   🦇   🦇

At 10 a.m. sharp, Sunday morning, Ivy convened the final meeting of Operation FANGED in Olivia's family room. Camilla, Olivia, Sophia and Brendan were all in attendance.

Ivy paced back and forth on the Abbott's blue shag carpet in front of the couch, where the others were all sitting in their sweats.

'We have exactly eight hours to plan and execute Dad's going-away party,' Ivy said. 'Synchronise watches.'

186

Everyone looked at their wrists except Brendan.

'I forgot my watch,' he winced. 'But I can use my cell phone.'

Ivy frowned at him in mock seriousness. 'You'd better shape up, Daniels, or you'll be scraping cake plates at the end of the night!' She surveyed the group. 'Now, to the first order of business: guests. At present time, we have none. We need invitations, and we need them fast. Any volunteers?'

Camilla's hand shot into the air. 'I can design something on Olivia's parents' computer,' she said, gesturing to the desk in the corner.

'Go!' Ivy commanded, and Camilla raced across the room.

Sophia raised her hand. Ivy pointed to her.

'Why are you acting like you're in a bad action movie about a SWAT team?' Sophia asked. Olivia and Brendan both chuckled.

'Because I'm moving to Europe in three days and I can do whatever I want,' Ivy said with a straight face. She cracked a smile. 'Also, I found these cargo pants while I was packing, and I think they look deadly.'

'They are pretty awesome,' Olivia agreed.

'Now,' Ivy continued, 'who wants to deliver invitations and spread the word as quickly as possible?'

'Brendan and I can do it,' said Sophia. 'We can run faster than, you know, most people.'

'I used to do track!' Camilla volunteered from where she was sitting at the computer.

But Ivy knew what Sophia meant – vampires were just superior to humans when it came to strength and speed. 'Don't you worry, Edmunson,' she told Camilla, 'there will be more than enough tasks to go around. Besides, we only have you until 1400 hours.' Camilla was hosting a big online forum for sci-fi geeks this evening, so she wasn't going to be able to attend the party – which was probably for the best, since it was going to be Vamp Central.

'The next thing we need,' Ivy went on, 'is a guest list. We want as many of my father's friends and acquaintances as can possibly make it at such short notice. Abbott – pen and paper?'

'Check,' said Olivia, holding them up.

'Commence brainstorming!' Ivy declared.

Everyone started calling out names, and Olivia scribbled them down furiously. In fifteen minutes, they had a list of almost seventy-five people.

'Wow!' said Olivia, flexing her aching hand. 'Your dad's almost as popular as you, Ivy.'

Camilla rushed over with a sheet from the printer and handed it to Ivy. It was a jet-black square with white text and an icon of a white airplane on it.

'"You are cordially invited,"' Ivy read aloud, '"to bid fond farewell to Charles Vega before he departs Franklin Grove for exciting opportunities abroad."' She flicked the paper with a black fingernail. 'Excellent work, Edmunson! Let's print one hundred copies and put them in the hands of our invitation runners ASAVP.'

'You mean ASAP?' said Camilla.

Oops, thought Ivy. She'd mistakenly used the acronym for 'As Soon As Vampirically Possible'. 'Yes,' she replied.

Sophia and Brendan put on their coats, and the moment the invitations had finished printing, they rushed out of the door to deliver them.

'What else can I do?' asked Camilla eagerly.

Olivia flipped through her notes. She looked up: 'We need to get to FoodMart to pick up paper plates and cups.'

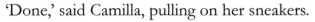

'Done,' said Camilla, pulling on her sneakers.

After Camilla left, Olivia tossed Ivy the phone and she dialled the number for the BloodMart.

'Catering Manager, please,' Ivy requested. 'Hi, Mr Bobovitch, it's Ivy Vega. I'm calling because we're throwing a last-minute surprise going-away party for my father tonight.' She ordered a bunch of finger foods to be delivered to her house that evening. 'And I hope you can make it too, Mr Bobovitch,' she added. 'My father has always said you're the best caterer outside of Transylvania. And pass the invitation along to anyone else you think might like to come.'

'Will do, Ivy,' Mr Bobovitch answered. 'Everyone was saddened to hear that your father is leaving us. I know lots of folks will want to say goodbye.'

Ivy hung up and handed the phone back to her sister. 'What's next?'

Olivia glanced at her notebook. 'Now that invites and catering are taken care of, the only thing left is decorating your house. We can meet there this afternoon. If we work together, it shouldn't take more than a couple of hours.'

'That won't work,' Ivy realised. 'Dad's going to be home all day packing.'

Olivia wrinkled her nose. 'How are we supposed to throw him a surprise party if we can't surprise him?'

Ivy pursed her lips thoughtfully. 'This calls for a covert operation.' A plan came together in her mind. 'Later this afternoon, you and I will go to my house, and you'll sneak around the back. You'll hide in my room while I convince my dad to take me to the mall. I'll keep him away until 7 p.m., when all the guests should be there.'

'Great,' Olivia approved. 'That gives Brendan, Sophia and me about two hours to get everything ready.' She stood up from the couch and saluted Ivy. Ivy saluted back, and they both cracked up.

🦇 　　　🦇　　　　🦇

They had a few hours to kill before going to Ivy's house, so Olivia invited her sister down to the kitchen to have a bite for lunch. Her parents were out visiting friends who had just had a baby, so she and Ivy had the place to themselves.

Watching Ivy pick at a patty of raw ground beef while she had tuna salad, Olivia couldn't help marvelling at the differences between the two of them – and at how close they'd become.

'You know,' Ivy said, crumpling her napkin, 'there is one person who knows the whole truth about why our dad's moving.'

'Who?' Olivia asked.

'Him,' Ivy replied. She had a determined look in her eye. 'We have to confront our father, Olivia.'

'But what if he freaks out?' Olivia said. 'He might do something really drastic.'

Ivy raised her eyebrows. 'You mean like move to *Europe*?'

Good point, thought Olivia.

'What do we have to lose?' Ivy pressed.

Olivia searched her mind. 'Nothing,' she had to admit finally. *At the very least*, she thought, *he ought to know that I know he's my dad before he goes.*

'We'll do it tomorrow,' Ivy decided.

A sickly feeling crept into Olivia's stomach, but she tried to ignore it. 'OK,' she said, 'but in the meantime, let's focus on throwing him the best party ever.'

Later that afternoon, Olivia waited the agreed-upon five minutes before following her sister up the long drive to the house atop Undertaker Hill. In the hours since she and Ivy had decided to confront their father, Olivia hadn't been able to get rid of the queasy feeling in the pit of her stomach.

Maybe my father's not the only one who's scared of the truth, she thought.

She forced herself to put one moonboot in front of the other and started her climb up the frozen drive. Her duffel bag tugged at her shoulder. It was full of left-over decorations from the All Hallows' Ball. She crept around the back of the house, slid open Ivy's basement window, threw the bag in, and crawled inside. Hiding near the top of the basement stairs, she could hear Ivy and her father talking.

'But, Ivy, you are not being reasonable. You do not need me to take you to the mall,' Mr Vega was saying. 'I have to keep packing.'

'You have to take to me,' Ivy pleaded. 'I need . . . a book for the plane. And I'm out of toothpaste. And my bag is too small. I don't even have a ski suit!'

'But you do not ski,' Mr Vega said.

'You want me to go to boarding school without a ski suit?' Ivy cried, sounding hurt. Olivia had to bite her tongue to keep from laughing. 'This is our last chance for affordable prices, Dad. Once we get to Europe, it'll be nothing but expensive designer labels.'

'All right,' Mr Vega finally gave in. 'Allow me to get my keys.'

As soon as she heard the front door shut, Olivia hurried upstairs to start decorating. She almost dropped her poms when she saw the living room. It was completely taken over by boxes. They were everywhere: on the coffee table, on the couch, on all the chairs. The floor was so crowded that there was barely any place to put down her duffel bag.

Olivia had no choice: she was going to have to stack all the boxes against one wall to make room for the party. Maybe they could put a banner or something on the front of them so they didn't make the room look untidy.

She pushed up her sleeves and got to work. Before long, she'd built a tower of boxes that was as tall as she was against the wall. She pushed it gently with her hand to see if it was stable. *One more small box on top*, she decided, scanning the floor.

She spotted one that was just the right size and waded over. When she bent down, though, it was so heavy she could barely lift it. *What's in here?* she wondered. She found the word 'LIBRARY' written on one side in black magic marker.

Olivia got her fingers underneath the box's edges and lifted with her legs. 'Urgh!' she groaned. It was like carrying a boulder. By the time she finally made it back across the room to her box tower, she felt like her arms were going to come off. She shut her eyes and gave three quick breaths. Then she hoisted the box over her head like a weight-lifter. Her arms quaked violently.

I did it! she thought.

Suddenly, the box's weight shifted and she felt it slipping from her hands. 'Whoooaaa!' The box fell to the floor with a crash. It burst open and its contents spilled everywhere.

'Well, I *almost* did it,' Olivia said to herself. With a sigh, she bent down to clean up the mess. She picked up a small wooden box and turned it over.

It was the box she and Ivy had discovered in their father's private collection, the one with the wedding-day photo of their parents. Then Olivia's eyes fell on a small black book that had

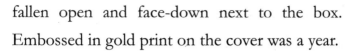

fallen open and face-down next to the box. Embossed in gold print on the cover was a year.

The year we were born, Olivia realised with a shock.

She picked up the book, turned it over, and was confronted by line after line of tight, graceful handwriting. The first entry was dated not long after she and Ivy were born. Olivia started reading.

> *I feel as if I am buried underground without the benefit of a coffin, trapped in the dark without hope of returning to see the light. Susannah was my sunshine. And it is my fault, my fault alone, that her beautiful light no longer shines upon this earth.*

What does he mean it's his fault? Olivia wondered. She saw her own name farther down.

From the night they came — our daughters, Olivia and Ivy — I see Susannah's beauty in their faces. But what if they are as doomed as our love? I know now that there is reason behind the madness of the old legends, about the monstrous consequences of a human and vampire loving one another.

With trembling fingers, Olivia turned the page.

Susannah was killed bringing our daughters into this world. Her human body could not cope with vampire blood running in her veins. Olivia and Ivy are not the monsters. They are the angels. It is I who am the monster. I chose to flout the old traditions, and Susannah has suffered the consequence.

I can not undo the evil I have done. But I vow to raise our daughters with the same supreme love that Susannah showed me. My soul may not be saved, but I shall do everything in my power to save theirs.

Olivia set the book down and closed her eyes. She needed a moment to digest what she'd just read. *Our mother didn't die in an accident like the Andover obituary said,* she realised. *She died in childbirth. And our father blamed himself.* Still, it was clear that he hadn't wanted to separate Ivy and Olivia at first. He'd wanted to raise them together. *So what happened?*

Olivia quickly leafed through the journal. A lot of it was about raising a human and a vampire infant side-by-side – 'Olivia tried to drink from Ivy's bottle today, and I was terrified.' And every few paragraphs, there seemed to be another mention of their mother, and her death. Her father's guilt seemed to get worse and worse.

Finally, Olivia came to the final entry, dated the day before her first birthday. She took a deep breath.

For a year, I have fooled myself into believing that I could safely raise Olivia and Ivy together. Their mother died because human and vampire mixed – could there be greater evidence of the horrors that await them if they remain together? And yet I have forced them to live as twin souls, against sense, against nature, because I needed comfort in my sorrow.

I fear for Olivia most of all. Even if she could grow up in my home without incident, there is no way the Blood Secret could be kept from her. She will live her life among vampires. One day, she may want a husband. She will disregard my warnings about mixing, just as I disregarded my parents' warnings.

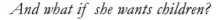

And what if she wants children?

I swear upon Susannah's grave that I shall not make the same mistake twice. I must give up Olivia so that she can be raised in a human family. I love her more than my heart can bear. My soul screams out against leaving her, but I will not allow my selfishness to endanger her. Not any more.

A clear droplet splattered on the page, and Olivia realised that she was crying. She put down the book, and let the tears run down her face. *He isn't moving to get away from me*, she thought. *He's trying to protect me.* She smiled through her tears. *He loves me! My father loves me.*

She turned to the very last page of the journal, where there were only a few lines, followed by an expanse of blank page.

I would rather tell Ivy she is adopted than ever reveal my terrible secrets. She will never know of her mother. She will never know of her sister. It is our only hope of putting the past behind us. It is the best I can do for our daughters, and the least I can do for my Susannah, may she rest in eternal peace.

Olivia closed the book and rested her head on the side of the box. *I wish Ivy were here*, she thought desperately. She thought about calling her on her cell, but she couldn't give Ivy news like this when she was at the mall with her dad.

The doorbell rang, and Olivia looked at her watch. *It's Sophia and Brendan*, she realised with a shock. She quickly wiped her face on the sleeve of her shirt and shoved the journal, the wooden box, and the other library things into the packing box from which they'd spilled.

'Hey. Are you OK?' Sophia asked when Olivia opened the front door.

'You look like you've been crying,' Brendan noted.

It wouldn't be fair to tell them before Ivy, Olivia decided. 'Must be all the dust,' Olivia shrugged, wiping her nose. She forced herself back into the party spirit. 'I was just moving packing boxes against the wall in the living room. Come on in. We have a lot of decorating to do!'

❤   ❤   ❤

As Ivy's father drove up their driveway, Ivy glanced at the clock on the dashboard: 7:05 p.m. *I hope people have actually shown up*, she thought nervously. *And I hope my dad won't be mad at me for inviting so many people to our house!*

Once they'd parked, her father went around and opened the trunk, which was filled with shopping bags. 'Well,' he said, 'I should think you now have everything you need for Europe.'

'Thanks, Dad,' Ivy said. He looped his arms with shopping bags, and climbed the front steps. Ivy hurried in front of him and said, 'I'll get it.'

She slowly opened the door for him, and he walked into the darkened foyer ahead of her. Suddenly, Ivy saw him tense, like something was wrong. 'Ivy,' he said quickly, 'is there something –'

'SURPRISE!' a chorus of voices shouted from the darkness, and Ivy's dad was so startled he dropped all of her bags.

The lights came on, revealing that the entire front foyer and first flight of the grand staircase were filled with guests. Olivia was perched on the end of one of the balustrades, with a party hat on her head.

Ivy's father was speechless. He sputtered and

stuttered, but couldn't get anything out. Finally he turned around in shock. 'Did you know this was happening?' he asked Ivy.

'It was my idea,' Ivy smiled. Her dad's eyes softened, but before he could say anything else, the crowd descended on him, slapping his back and shaking his hand.

Ivy scanned the room. It seemed like every vampire in Franklin Grove had shown up – and then some! There was Mr Grosvenor from the museum, and Vincent the Butcher, and Dr Pane Lee, their dentist. Georgia Huntingdon from *Vamp!* had flown in specially for the occasion. Alice Bantam was there, wearing what looked like galoshes and a yellow and grey plastic bag. Even Miss Everling had made it! Ivy spotted Brendan, standing with his parents and Bethany on the other side of the room, and waved to him. He gave her a big, proud thumbs up. In return, she blew him a kiss. He caught it right on the neck.

Suddenly, the crowd started calling, 'Speech! Speech!' and Ivy joined in.

'Yes, yes,' her father said, raising his hands in the air. 'Keep your fangs in.'

Everybody laughed.

'I would like to begin by thanking my beautiful daughter, Ivy, for planning this.' The room burst into applause, and Ivy couldn't help beaming. 'And I would like to thank all of you for coming,' her father continued. 'But more than that, I would like to thank each and every one of you for welcoming me from the day I arrived in this town. Franklin Grove will always be my home. And I will always think of you, all of you, as my family.' His voice choked up. 'It breaks my heart to leave you.'

People said 'Aw,' and cheered.

'Enjoy the party!' her father called.

Ivy noticed that, over on the balustrade, Olivia was clapping but her mouth was trembling between a smile and a frown.

Chapter Ten

Olivia saw her sister making her way towards her through the crowd of guests. She hopped down from her perch and met her halfway. They shared a hug.

'The house looks drops dead,' Ivy told her.

'I have to talk to you,' Olivia said seriously. She was about to go on, but she noticed their dad approaching. He came up behind Ivy and gave her a hug.

'I know how hard it has been for you to accept this move,' Mr Vega said. 'It makes me all the more grateful that you went to all this trouble.'

'Olivia helped too,' Ivy said. 'I couldn't have done it without her.'

Mr Vega took a tentative step towards Olivia. He took a deep breath and abruptly threw his arms around her. 'Thank you, Olivia,' he said.

'Not so tight,' Olivia squeaked.

Her father released her at once. 'Have I hurt you?' he asked in a panic.

'I'm fine,' she assured him. *He's so worried about harming me*, she thought tenderly.

'Charles!' waved Georgia Huntingdon from where she was chatting with Mr Grosvenor on a chaise longue in the corner. Their father smiled at the girls, his eyes sparkling, before heading off to mingle with more of his guests.

Olivia took her sister's hand and led her through the crowd, to the alcove off the front hall with the grand piano. Luckily, it was deserted.

'I found something while I was setting up,'

Olivia whispered to her sister. 'Our father's journal from right after we were born.'

Ivy's black-lined eyes searched Olivia's face. 'And?'

'And our mother died giving birth to us,' Olivia said. She could feel her heart beating in her chest.

Ivy squinted, like she was trying to see through a dense fog.

'Our dad thought that her body couldn't cope with having vampire blood inside her,' Olivia explained.

Ivy's knees buckled slightly, and she collapsed on the piano bench. She looked confused, but she didn't say anything.

'That's why he wanted to separate us,' Olivia went on. 'He thought the same thing would happen to me if I hung around vampires. He was worried I'd fall in love with one or something. I guess he still is. That's why he feels you should both move away.'

'But that makes no sense,' Ivy shook her head. 'It's not as if you're getting a blood transfusion. We just want to be sisters. We just want to go to school together.'

'I know that,' Olivia said. 'But he's the one we have to convince.'

Ivy stood up, her eyes clear. 'Let's do it now,' she said. 'I can't pretend to be having fun when all of this has come up from the grave.'

Olivia nodded, and together they went to go and find their dad.

🦇 🦇 🦇

'Dad, can I talk to you?' Ivy said. She and her sister had finally found him in the kitchen, talking animatedly to Rafe, the coffin carpenter.

'Sure,' he smiled, gesturing for Ivy to say whatever was on her mind.

'In private?' Ivy clarified.

Her dad looked puzzled, but then he saw Olivia standing at Ivy's side, noticed the looks on the girls' faces, and his expression changed to one of concern. 'Of course,' he said quickly and set his drink on the counter. 'Pardon me, Rafe. Let us go up to my study,' he suggested to the girls.

The journey through the house and up the stairs to the second floor felt like it took an eternity to Ivy. Every few feet, someone stopped her father and wanted to chat. Finally, the three of them reached the study. Her father shut the door and went and sat in his office chair.

'Is everything all right?' he asked.

This is it, thought Ivy. 'We know,' she said simply.

A series of reactions crossed her father's face: shock, then panic, followed by denial. 'You know what?' he shrugged unconvincingly.

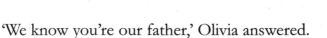

'We know you're our father,' Olivia answered.

'And we know about our mom, too,' Ivy finished.

Her father stared at them in disbelief. 'But how . . .' he stammered.

'We found your wedding photo,' Ivy explained.

'And the journal you kept,' added Olivia.

Their dad searched their faces, his eyes fluttering frantically from Ivy to her sister. Ivy could tell he was desperately trying to figure out what to say. For a second, a crooked smile revealed his teeth, and she knew he was tempted to deny everything. But then the smile disappeared, and a pained look was all that remained.

'You know everything?' he whispered. Ivy and Olivia nodded, and their father closed his eyes. Suddenly he breathed in sharply, as if he had been punched in the stomach.

'I loved your mother so very much.' He was

holding his breath, his voice high and strained. 'I didn't think I could live,' he swallowed. 'The only thing that kept me in this world . . . was the two of you.' All at once, he slumped in his chair and tears streamed from his eyes. He put his face in his hands and wept.

Ivy felt like she was watching her own father be reduced to dust. It was awful. She and Olivia reached out, but he raised his hands, gesturing for them to stay back so he could go on.

'My parents always told me that vampires and humans shouldn't mix,' he explained. 'But the moment I met Susannah, your mother, I knew at once she was the only woman for me. I didn't care that she was human.' He wiped the tears from his eyes roughly with the palms of his hands. 'When she told me she was pregnant, I thought it was a miracle. I had believed – everyone believed – that that just wasn't possible. I thought it was proof of the extraordinary power of our love.' He shook his head forlornly. 'I could not have been more wrong.'

'She died in labour?' Olivia said.

'She died,' her father answered soberly, 'because of me. I never should have let her love me. My parents were right – vampires and humans should not mix. It only brings tragedy.'

He levelled his eyes at Ivy. 'You see now, my darling, why we must move?'

'But the Vampire Round Table –' Olivia began.

'My dear Olivia, my beautiful daughter,' he interrupted, turning his hopeless eyes on her. 'Yes, the Vampire Round Table accepts you. But that does not make you one of us. I could not believe it when I learned you had come to Franklin Grove. It was certainly destiny for you and Ivy to find each other.' He sighed. 'I suppose, somewhere deep inside, I wanted it to happen. I left you both our rings. But I could not bear to lose you the way I lost Susannah,' he said hoarsely. 'That is why we must be apart.' He rapped the desk with his fist, like a judge decreeing his decision.

Ivy wanted to say something to convince her father that everything would be OK. Except now she wasn't so sure herself. *What if something horrible does happen to Olivia if we stay together?* she thought. *After all, it was my embryo's blood that infected our mom.* Olivia's hand slipped from her own, and the three of them were silent, lost in their own thoughts.

Then their father turned his chair away and gently asked them to leave him be for a moment. Ivy and her sister walked slowly out of the room. There seemed to be nothing left to say.

🦇　　　🦇　　　🦇

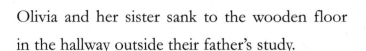

Olivia and her sister sank to the wooden floor in the hallway outside their father's study.

'It wasn't his fault,' Olivia said softly.

'You're right,' Ivy said, a curtain of hair shielding her face. 'It was mine.'

'What?' Olivia asked in surprise.

'You were the human baby,' Ivy explained sadly. 'I was the vampire. Our mother died from having me.'

'Ivy, that's not true,' Olivia protested. Her sister looked at her doubtfully out of the corner of her eye. 'Brendan's father said the human and vampire cells polarised. After that it would have been a normal pregnancy.'

Ivy shook her head. 'We don't know that.'

Our father spent the last thirteen years blaming himself for our mother's death, Olivia thought. *I can't let Ivy make the same mistake.* She stood up and held out her hand. 'Come on.'

'Where are we going?' Ivy asked, allowing herself to be pulled to her feet.

'To find Mr Daniels,' Olivia told her. 'We're going to get this straightened out once and for all.'

They spotted Brendan's dad in the living room, talking to a short pale man in sunglasses. 'Sorry, can we pry you away for a minute?' Olivia asked.

Mr Daniels followed them into the kitchen. 'Ivy and I have something to ask you,' Olivia said.

'Of course,' Mr Daniels replied. Ivy bit her lip and stared down at her boots.

'Could a human woman die from giving birth to a vampire?' blurted Olivia.

'It depends,' Mr Daniels answered, and Olivia felt a flicker of worry.

'On what?' she risked.

'Mainly on whether she kept up her iron

intake,' replied Mr Daniels. 'But, assuming a balanced diet, there's no reason a human mother couldn't act as a surrogate to a vampire child. Why do you ask?'

'Because we found out that our mother died in childbirth,' Olivia explained plainly. She looked over at her sister, and it was clear Ivy still wasn't convinced. 'Could she have died because she needed more iron or whatever?'

'No, no, that wouldn't have been the situation in your case,' Mr Daniels replied, shaking his wild mane of grey hair.

Ivy looked up. 'Why not?'

'Because iron deficiency in the mother would almost certainly result in birth defects in the vampire offspring, and you're healthy as a bat. The normal, human complications that often arise during labour were probably the cause of your mother's death.'

'So it wasn't having me as a daughter?' Ivy enquired softly.

Mr Daniels squeezed Ivy's shoulder affectionately. 'No,' he said. 'Certainly not,' he added more forcefully.

Olivia saw relief wash over her sister's face. 'Thanks, Mr Daniels,' Olivia said triumphantly.

🦇 🦇 🦇

Ivy felt like she'd just had a blood transfusion. 'Would you be willing to tell my father what you just said?' she asked.

He looked puzzled. 'I suppose so, but why?'

Ivy exchanged glances with her sister. *We have to tell Brendan's father the truth*, Ivy thought, shepherding him further into the corner by the pantry, so no one else would overhear. 'If we tell you a secret,' Ivy said, 'will you promise to keep it?'

Mr Daniels paused, studying the serious

expressions on Ivy and Olivia's faces. 'I will,' he pledged finally.

'Remember when you told us about Karl Lazar,' Ivy said, 'the vamp who fell in love with a human and went into hiding?'

'Yes,' Mr Daniels agreed.

'Well, we found him,' Olivia whispered.

'You did?' Mr Daniels' eyes widened. 'Where?'

'In Franklin Grove,' Ivy replied. 'He changed his name to Charles Vega.'

'Inconceivable!' Mr Daniels gasped.

'But true,' said Ivy. 'My dad is our *real* dad. And he thinks our mother died because he got her pregnant with a vampire baby.'

Thankfully, Mr Daniels understood at once why the girls wanted him to speak to their father. 'Lead the way!' he said.

Ivy knocked lightly on the study door. 'Dad?'

'You may enter,' his voice came faintly.

'Dad, Mr Daniels is here.' Brendan's father followed her into the room, and Olivia came in behind him. 'He has something to tell you.'

'Your wife's death was not your fault, Charles,' Mr Daniels said simply.

Her father bristled. 'I appreciate your concern, Marc, but –'

Mr Daniels put up his hand. 'Let me finish. I have been studying human/vampire childbirth for nearly a decade, and your daughters' particular case around the clock for two weeks. When the girls' mother was impregnated, the human cells and vampire cells separated and formed two entirely distinct embryos. From that moment on, the pregnancy would have been completely normal. All of my research confirms this. There would have been no toxic effects from the vampire DNA in your wife's womb.'

'Then what killed her?' Ivy's father demanded.

'Human medicine and science have greatly advanced,' Mr Daniels said. 'But even now, in this day and age, there are unpreventable fatalities during childbirth. It is the way of nature. It is *human* nature, Marc.' Mr Daniels spread his hands. 'It has nothing to do with vampires.'

Something changed in Mr Vega's eyes. 'Are you sure?' he asked, his voice faltering.

'I am as sure as a geneticist can be,' Mr Daniels said gently.

Charles Vega rose slowly from his desk and came around to stand before Mr Daniels. Then, to Ivy's amazement, he threw his arms around Brendan's father. 'Thank you,' he gasped. 'Thank you.'

'You are most welcome,' Mr Daniels replied generously.

Ivy's father turned to face her. Beaming, he grabbed her hand. With the other, he took Olivia's.

'Can the two of you ever forgive me?' he asked. 'For deceiving you for so long? For being so wrong?'

Olivia's lip was trembling. 'As long as you promise to forgive yourself,' she said tenderly. 'Dad,' she added with a gulp.

Their father pulled the two of them to his chest, and Ivy looked across to see Olivia smiling at her with tears in her eyes. She heard Mr Daniels let himself quietly out of the study.

Ivy hugged her sister and her father as tightly as she could. For the first time, there weren't any secrets to keep the three of them apart.

Chapter Eleven

'I'm dreaming of a *black* Christmas,' Olivia sang to herself as she painted her nails frosted pink. It was Christmas Eve, and her sister was rummaging around in the bottom of her closet, checking to see whether Olivia had any shoes that might match the outfit she was planning on wearing for tomorrow's Christmas dinner.

Their dad's party – and all the emotions that had gone along with it – was just last night. But it seemed like ages ago.

'Did you see the look on my dad's face when

your parents invited us for Christmas dinner?'
Ivy said.

'Totally,' Olivia nodded. She blew on her toes.
'He was, like, all mushy.'

Charles and Ivy had brought Olivia home
after the party, and Olivia had been completely
impressed with the way he had come clean
about everything to her parents – except the
vampire stuff, of course. He was just like, 'I'm
Olivia's biological father, but you're still her
parents, and I'm sorry I wasn't honest the
moment Ivy and Olivia found each other.' It was
really brave of him. Olivia's mom and dad were
amazing, too – they took the news so graciously.
And the best part?

'I still can't believe we're not moving,' said Ivy,
examining the heels on a pair of dark pumps. 'It's
like I just woke up from a bad dream.'

'That's funny,' said Olivia. 'Because I feel like

I fell asleep and am having the best dream ever!'
When Ivy and their dad left, she and her
parents had had a little celebratory freak out in
the living room about the fact that Ivy was
staying. They had jumped up and down and
hugged. It was cute.

'Now this is what I've been looking for,' Ivy
announced. She held up a pair of fire-engine-
red heels.

'Those are definitely *not* black,' Olivia noted.

'I thought I'd add a little colour,' Ivy grinned.

Olivia chuckled. 'So what do you want to
do today?'

'I don't know,' Ivy shrugged. 'Now that I
don't have to finish packing, we can do whatever
we want.'

'I feel like we've been so busy trying to keep
you from having to move,' Olivia said, 'that I
barely noticed it was the holidays. I *love* Christmas.'

The smiling image of Santa Claus on a Christmas card pinned to the bulletin board by the door caught Olivia's eye, and suddenly she had an idea. She was so excited that she waved at the air with her still-wet fingertips spread wide. 'I know! We can go see the HB!'

Ivy groaned. 'Olivia, we're too old.'

'You're just saying that because you grew up with it. But I've never been to meet the Holiday Bat. Don't you think that's sad?'

'No,' Ivy said. 'What's sad is going to see the HB when you're thirteen!'

'Come on,' Olivia pleaded. 'It's the perfect thing to do on Christmas Eve. Please, Ivy.'

'OK, but you can bet I'm not going to suffer through this alone,' Ivy qualified, whipping out her cell phone.

Olivia's mom gave them a ride, and Brendan and Sophia were waiting for them outside

Kruller's Department Store. They pretty much tackled Ivy as soon as she and Olivia got out of the car.

'You're not moving?' Sophia cried, grabbing Ivy's arms.

'I'm not moving!' Ivy beamed.

'You're staying,' Brendan whispered, pulling her close and breathing into her hair.

'She's staying!' Olivia repeated, adding a little *whoop* for good measure.

They stood outside taking turns hugging each other until Brendan pulled open the door for everyone.

'I haven't seen the HB in three blue moons,' said Sophia.

'How long's that?' asked Olivia.

'Since we were six,' Ivy answered.

'Olivia, if you're going to be hanging with the black cats,' Sophia teased, swinging her camera expertly by its strap, 'you have to learn the lingo.'

'Oh, yeah? Put a stake in it,' Olivia said with mock Goth chilliness.

'Oooooh! Snap!' said Brendan. Her vampire friends laughed, impressed by Olivia's comeback.

Arm in arm, the four of them made their way through the bustling holiday crowds and down the main aisle of the department store. Eventually they came to an elevator near the back. 'Here we are,' said Brendan.

Olivia couldn't believe it. *Kruller's is a vampire establishment?* she thought. *I just bought a gorgeous hot-pink miniskirt here last month!*

The elevator door opened with a *ding*, and the four of them squeezed inside with a bunch of other shoppers. Sophia hit the button for five, the top floor. On their way up, a few people got off on each floor. Finally, the door opened on five, and the few remaining passengers walked out.

Olivia started to follow, but Ivy grabbed her arm and gave her a meaningful look. The doors closed.

Ivy reached over and shifted the 'IN CASE OF EMERGENCY' sign beside the door, revealing an alpha-numeric keypad. She punched in a series of numbers, and a small metal panel automatically slid open to show a single round elevator button with an upside down V on it. Ivy pushed it, and the button glowed green.

'Going down,' Sophia announced.

Olivia watched the LED display over the door that showed what floor they were on. It fell from five to one in a matter of seconds, and then it read 'B' for basement. Then the B disappeared, and the lights went out in the elevator, plunging Olivia and her friends into complete darkness.

Brendan wailed spookily like a ghost. Olivia could feel the car continuing to plunge downwards. *How much lower can we go?* she wondered. *What if we crash into the bottom?*

'Guys?' she said tentatively.

Suddenly, the car jolted to a stop, and Olivia almost fell over. *Ding*: the red LED over the door showed an upside down V, and the door slid open.

Olivia could not believe her eyes. There was a whole other department store down here, and it was packed with Goths doing their last-minute holiday shopping!

'Welcome to Cruellers,' Brendan said in tour guide mode, 'the third largest vamp shopping destination in North America.'

'I knew you guys had your own parts of stores, but this is . . .' Olivia searched for the right word, her head spinning with all the vampires and amazing vampire stuff around her. 'It's *vampalicious*!'

'Vampalicious!' Ivy repeated, rolling the word with her tongue. Her mouth curled into a devilish grin.

They made their way into the cosmetics department, passing a counter featuring 'Twenty-three Different Shades of Pale'. Olivia looked on with interest as an aesthetician applied black lipstick to a pale-faced customer in a nurse's uniform. An elegant vamp stepped towards them with a spray bottle. 'Would you like to try some *Decomposure*?' the woman offered.

'No, thanks,' Olivia gawked.

They crossed into Ladies' Fashion. On a table checkered with folded T-shirts, Olivia spotted one with an icon of an upside-down bunny rabbit that had Xs instead of eyes. She grabbed it and pressed it to her chest.

'I so have to have this,' she said.

'Are you kidding?' Sophia said, snatching

the T-shirt away from her. 'That's a Paul Frankenstein. It costs a fortune!'

People kept whispering and staring at them as they passed. Olivia assumed it was because of her sherpa jacket and moonboots. After all, it's not every day that a cheerleader bounces through a vamp department store. But then, as they were entering the toy department, a little black-haired girl in red glasses came up to them, with her mother standing not far behind.

'Are you Olivia and Ivy?' the little girl asked shyly.

Olivia and her sister both nodded. 'We sure are,' Olivia admitted.

'Can I have your autograph for my friend?' the girl asked, holding out a piece of paper and a pen.

Right, we're almost famous, Olivia remembered. She took the pen and smiled. 'What's your friend's name?'

'Clarissa,' the girl said shyly. 'She's a human. She doesn't know about vampires. But we both have pictures of you up in our rooms.'

'And what's your name?'

'Erica,' said the girl.

'Dear Clarissa,' Olivia wrote in script. 'You and Erica are vampalicious.' That word looked good on paper, too. 'Love, Olivia.'

Olivia passed the piece of paper to Ivy, who added, 'PS That means you suck.'

'Just tell her it's Goth slang,' Olivia told Erica, who grabbed the paper and ran to show her mother.

Olivia and her friends walked on. 'There's the HB,' Brendan announced suddenly. Olivia looked around, but she didn't see anything that looked like a Holiday Bat.

Then she looked up. The vaulted ceiling was so high it disappeared into darkness, and up there, in the air, was a huge bat flying in circles, its wings flapping energetically. There were three children on its back, squealing happily.

Olivia quickened her step, and soon she found a sign that said 'To the Holiday Bat Hideaway'. A line of people snaked past it, and she realised that there were already dozens of children and their parents waiting for their turn on the HB.

'Come on!' Olivia said, dragging her sister down the aisle to get in line.

🦇   🦇   🦇

'This is taking eternity,' Ivy groaned. They'd already been waiting for twenty minutes, and they still weren't close to the front of the line.

Olivia didn't even seem to hear her, though. She was staring up at the HB with her mouth hanging open and her eyes glazed over. The people in front of them took a few steps forward. Ivy, Sophia and Brendan did the same, but Olivia didn't move, leaving a gap in the line.

'Take three steps forward, Batgirl,' Sophia said. Olivia obediently shuffled up without lowering her eyes.

An unsmiling guy wearing goggles and fuzzy black wings on his back walked by for the millionth time. 'Please turn off all cell phones so as not to interfere with the HB's holidaytime radar,' he said loudly. 'Please tie all shoelaces and remove all scarves.' Ivy rolled her eyes at Brendan and saw him mouthing the guy's words. 'Please do not bring food or blood on the HB.' She cracked up.

'What's the story behind it?' Olivia said reverently. 'Like, does it live at the North Pole?'

'Nope,' said Sophia. 'It lives everywhere there's darkness. In the days leading up to Christmas, little vampires everywhere whisper what they want out of the window. The Holiday

Bat, being a bat, has extraordinary hearing.'

'You don't have to make a list?' Olivia asked. 'You just whisper what you want for Christmas?'

'Exactly,' Sophia confirmed. 'Only humans would come up with something as boring as writing a list for the holidays. Everything's a chore with you people.'

'That's such a stereotype!' Olivia protested.

'Said the cheerleader to the vampire,' Brendan laughed.

Ivy burst out laughing too at that. She gave Brendan a peck on the cheek for being utterly charming.

Finally, they arrived at the front of the line. Two more humourless people in goggles ushered them up to the HB, which had just landed.

'Who would like to sit at the front?' one of them asked.

Olivia's hand shot into the air. 'I would! I would!' she cried excitedly. Brendan and Sophia climbed on behind her.

'There's room for one more,' announced one of the HB helpers.

'Let's go, Ivy,' Olivia called.

'I'm OK,' Ivy answered. 'I'd rather keep my feet on the ground.'

'Come *on*,' Olivia and Brendan and Sophia all chided. 'You have to!'

'No thanks,' Ivy repeated.

'Ivy! Ivy! Ivy!' her friends started chanting. And, suddenly, the people behind Ivy began to join in.

Ivy threw her arms in the air. 'All right! I'm going!' Some of the people in line actually cheered.

Ivy squeezed on to the bat's back, right behind Olivia. Brendan slid his arms comfortably around her waist. Sophia sat at the back.

With a lurch, the bat lifted into the air. Ivy shrieked and grabbed her sister's shoulders to steady herself. They began to climb higher and higher.

Brendan's arms tightened warmly around her, and soon they were swooping through the air, high above the crowd. Ivy closed her eyes and felt the wind blowing through her hair. Olivia's whoops of laughter filled her ears, and Ivy was overcome with joy. *I'm riding the HB*, she thought, *with my best friend, my boyfriend, and my sister. Now* that's *vampalicious!*

Squeezing Olivia's shoulders, she bent her head downwards. 'I wish,' Ivy whispered inaudibly to the bat beneath her, 'that I will always be surrounded by the people I love.' She knew the HB heard her wish. After all, it had extraordinary hearing, as all bats do.

Sink your teeth into this!

Being a new girl sucks. But then Olivia Abbot meets her long-lost twin sister, Ivy. They're as different as day and night – and Ivy has a grave secret. But it won't stop them getting to know each other's worlds. After all, blood is thicker than water – and it's certainly tastier!

Sink your teeth into the second book starring Olivia and Ivy

MY
SISTER THE VAMPIRE

FANGTASTIC!

Sienna Mercer

Since discovering her long-lost twin Ivy, Olivia is
learning about a whole new life. But the Franklin Grove
vampires can't let their secret get out and when the
journalist Serena Star starts to sniff around like
a bloodhound, the sisters must throw her off the scent.
This is one news story that can't see the light of day.

Sink your teeth into the third book starring Olivia and Ivy

The secret is out – Olivia and Ivy are twins! But some people are turning in their coffins about it. Ivy's adoptive dad doesn't believe Olivia won't betray the Franklin Grove vampires. To prove she can be trusted, Olivia must pass three tests – but not just any old tests. These are challenges to really get the blood pumping!

EGMONT PRESS: ETHICAL PUBLISHING

Egmont Press is about turning writers into successful authors and children into passionate readers – producing books that enrich and entertain. As a responsible children's publisher, we go even further, considering the world in which our consumers are growing up.

Safety First
Naturally, all of our books meet legal safety requirements. But we go further than this; every book with play value is tested to the highest standards – if it fails, it's back to the drawing-board.

Made Fairly
We are working to ensure that the workers involved in our supply chain – the people that make our books – are treated with fairness and respect.

Responsible Forestry
We are committed to ensuring all our papers come from environmentally and socially responsible forest sources.

For more information, please visit our website at
www.egmont.co.uk/ethicalpublishing

The Forest Stewardship Council (FSC) is an international, non-governmental organisation dedicated to promoting responsible management of the world's forests. FSC operates a system of forest certification and product labelling that allows consumers to identify wood and wood-based products from well-managed forests.

For more information about the FSC, please visit their website at www.fsc-uk.org

FSC
Mixed Sources
Product group from well-managed forests and other controlled sources

Cert no. TT-COC-2063
www.fsc.org
© 1996 Forest Stewardship Council